Friend of a Friend

A Joth Proctor Fixer Mystery

Books by James V. Irving

The Joth Proctor Fixer *series*
Friends Like These
Friend of a Friend
Friend of the Court

Friend of a Friend

A Joth Proctor Fixer Mystery

James V. Irving

SPEAKING VOLUMES, LLC
NAPLES, FLORIDA
2021

Friend of a Friend

ISBN 978-1-64540-485-9

For my parents, William Ralph Irving, M.D. and Marjorie Harrison Irving, with love and gratitude.

Acknowledgments

Thanks to four English teachers and mentors at Governor Dummer Academy - Elizabeth Baratelli, Chris Martin, John Ogden and Mac Murphy - who got me started; to my writing professors at the University of Virginia, Anne Freeman, Edward Jones and John Casey who showed me what's important and what's not, both in writing and in life; and to the faculty and staff at Shore Country Day School in Beverly, Mass., who instilled in me a love of fiction from an early age.

Thanks to my agent and wise counsel Nancy Rosenfeld; to my publisher Kurt Mueller, whose provided a steady hand at the tiller; and to the creative, energetic voice of my editor, David Tabatsky.

Colleagues and friends Scott Dondershine, Steve Moriarty and Tamar Abrams provided insight and practical advice that I couldn't have done without.

Thanks to Ken Willner, my buddy on F Dock.

I'd be remise not to acknowledge Gordon R. Butler and M. Morgan Cherry, my former employers at Legal Investigations, Inc., where real life adventure was frequently stranger than fiction.

Warm appreciation to my partners and co-workers at Bean, Kinney & Korman for their wit, insight, and store of legal knowledge, indispensable in both of my professions.

Thanks to my old roommate Joth Davis who graciously allowed me to borrow his name for use in this series.

A tip of the baseball cap to three jamokes who always seem to be around when I need them: Kevin Kearney, Peter Franklin and Paul Commito.

Thanks to two particularly supportive groups – and the two most consistently amusing groups of people I have ever been part of - my brethren at the Chi Psi Lodge at the University of Virginia and my old teammates at the Alexandria Lacrosse Club.

Particular thanks to my wife Cindy and daughter Lindsay without whom none of this would have been possible.

Chapter One

A Thin Connection

A smart lawyer once told me that smart lawyers don't represent their friends because they're likely to lose both the client and the friendship. I figured a friend of a friend is something else.

Not only was Halftrack Racker not a friend, he wasn't even a friend of the guy who referred him to me. By the time it was all over, Riley swore he hardly knew him.

I knew Track only casually. He'd been an All-American lacrosse player at the University of Virginia, a few years after my days there, and I'd been introduced to him at least a half dozen times over a span of more than a decade.

"You'll remember him," Riley said. "He's the big, red-headed guy with the long white scar across his jaw. Kind of crazy, but in a good way."

"I remember him."

Track wasn't crazy. He was merely nasty, in a brutish, unimaginative way, the kind of guy you wish you could forget.

"He would have been a good fit on your team," said Riley. "You guys, as good as you were, you could have used some brawn."

I didn't reply. Track was six-foot-three, rock solid, and built to knock people around. On the field, he would have been a great addition to any team, but his own teammates detested him, and mine wanted nothing to do with him. I suppose I held my own grudge against him, too, even after all these years. He embodied everything I held in contempt, as an athlete and a man.

Track lived just inside the Beltway in Old Town Alexandria, and for him, an early morning meeting in Arlington meant ten a.m. As soon as he entered my office, I felt a surge of revulsion, but I'm not in the habit of turning down clients.

He had a salesman's smile and a firm handshake, and he claimed to remember me from college, recalling goals I had no memory of scoring and specific details of several of our chance encounters, none of which were worth remembering, at least to me. His memory, and the way he shared it, as if he were already trying to create leverage with me, were both flattering and unsettling.

Track looked older, but not as old as I knew I did. He'd put on weight since I'd seen him last and he sported a ruddy colored, neatly trimmed beard that covered the jagged scar Riley had remembered on the phone. For a guy who never used to care much for appearances, Track now seemed to be all-in for such things. His blue suit had been tailored to flatter his imposing girth, and an ornate crucifix hung from a silver chain around his neck, nestling in his luxuriant chest hair. He had the look of a stock character out of a B-movie, but I couldn't recall which one.

I noticed him taking in my modest quarters with a look of pity and disdain. As he took a seat across from my desk, he dredged up name after name from years ago, what they were wearing at the time, what they had been drinking.

I couldn't have cared less.

"So," I said, trying to change the subject.

"You look good," he said hastily. "Handsomest guy on the midfield. That's what they used to say. Remember?"

If that had ever been true, which I doubted, it no longer was. The years had taken their toll, and I knew damn well that I looked more like an old warhorse than he did. I tried to keep in shape, but ever since I'd left 35 in the rearview mirror, it hadn't been so easy. A man's body has a mind of its own.

"I understand you have an insurance problem," I said, interrupting and shifting in my seat just enough to make him meet my gaze.

"I'm not sure it's really a problem, Joth."

"People don't normally come to see me unless they have a problem."

Track folded his heavy hands in his lap and immediately started working his stubby thumbs against each other.

"All right, you got me there. I've got a problem. Riley says you can fix it."

I nodded slightly and looked out the window, not wanting Track to take anything for granted. It was a damp and dreary early spring day, and the traffic was still backed up on Wilson Boulevard.

"There are a lot of people out there with more experience than me in insurance matters."

"Not this kind."

"Riley tell you that?"

Track put on the ingenuous grin of a college sophomore, as if it were something to connect us.

"Creative solutions to unique problems. That's what Riley said you're good at."

"I'll be sure to thank him."

He made a show of crossing his legs, revealing his hand-stitched cowboy boots, made from what appeared to have once been an exotic animal.

I shrugged.

"I'm a financial planner," he said.

"CFP?"

He frowned.

"Not exactly certified, no. I help people plan for retirement."

"How do you do that?"

"I get to know my clients, their families, and their needs," he said, beginning what sounded like a well-rehearsed sales pitch. "There are a lot of vehicles out there. I try to match my customers with the ones that will maximize their post-retirement security."

"Vehicles?"

"Annuities, sometimes. You know what an annuity is?"

"Yeah. It's a financial planning vehicle that does very well for the person selling it."

Track scowled.

"Or insurance policies. I handle those, too."

I nodded, as if that point made him sound more legit.

He paused and his eyebrows knitted together for a moment, and I wondered if he was about to reveal something.

"I find out what makes the most sense, from both a cost and ROI perspective. You know what I mean by ROI? Return on investment."

"Yes, I've heard of it."

He recrossed his legs and his top leg began to jiggle. He was nervous and I wondered why.

"So that's the kind of insurance problem we're talking about?" I said.

Track's hair was still thick and carrot colored. When he scratched at the part along one side, he produced a dusting of dandruff, which he quickly brushed away. Since my hair had been going gray for years, I was quietly gratified to see flecks of gray in his well-tended mane.

"I sold a customer of mine a life insurance policy. Then he won the lottery."

"Doesn't seem like much of a problem."

Track's head jerked up like a man who'd awakened to a surprising truth.

"You know what a viatical settlement is?"

That term struck a distantly familiar chord. It took me a moment to dial up a reasonable definition.

"It's when the insured person sells a policy on his life to a third party for a lump sum that's less than the death benefit," I said. "Something like that."

Track nodded.

"They're illegal in many states," I said.

"Not in Virginia," he said, a trace of a grin on his face. "If I recall correctly."

"I see," I said. "So, you arranged for your customer to sell a life insurance policy he no longer needed? Is that it?"

"Exactly."

"So, what's the problem?" I said.

"I bought the policy."

I took a breath before responding.

"I see," I said, looking back out the window.

I wasn't ready with a better reply because I was having difficulty containing my disgust. But if Track was right about the legality, I didn't see why he needed me, and besides a paycheck, I had no use for him. If I could've afforded to show him the door right then, I would have.

He sighed, as if he could sense my take on the whole mess.

"A financial planner can't own a policy on his client's life," he said. "It's against regulations, or something like that."

I nodded as I digested this nugget, making a mental note to remember it.

"What's the value of the policy?"

"Half a million bucks."

I whistled, which seemed to be the proper reaction.

"How did it come up in the first place?" I said.

"We were talking about his in-laws," said Track.

Track was a salesman. I watched him read my face. Blank as a barn door.

"He didn't literally win the lottery," he said. "His wife's uncle died and left her a bundle. But that can be the same thing."

"Did you know she was in line for a big inheritance when you sold him the policy?"

"We never discussed it until recently."

It was on the tip of my tongue to ask him how he advised a client to buy a life insurance policy without first understanding his wife's financial status, but I let it go. I already knew the answer.

"So, you suggested that . . ."

"I didn't really suggest it," he said. "Once I figured out who his wife was, and you'd recognize her maiden name, I told him we needed to talk. It's my job to make sure he's financially secure, and he is. I'm a straight shooter, Joth."

I waited for him to go on.

"That's why they call me Frank," he added, grinning.

Frank, I remembered, was Track's given name. He delighted in this lame pun, but the grin on his face affirmed my sense that Track wasn't the sort of person I wanted to take on as a client. I had the hunch that I was already in too deep.

"Listen Track . . ."

He cut me off, scowling menacingly, as if I had crossed a line.

"Don't call me that."

His response surprised me.

"It's your nickname. I mean, it has been for years."

It was appropriate, too. As a 20-year-old, he was built like a tank and moved like an agile assault vehicle, and he still looked dangerous, even with an extra layer of life packed on.

"Halftrack. That's where that comes from."

"Halftrack sounds like half-assed," he said. "That should have been your name."

"I didn't have a nickname," I said. "Lucky for me."

"You weren't good enough to have one."

For three years, I had run second midfield on the University of Virginia lacrosse team. My calling card has been crisp, solid play without a lot of flash or glory. In a moment of insight, I realized that Track remembered this and that's why he was in my office. Solid play without a lot of flash or glory—just what he needed, and at a price he could afford.

I slid a legal pad in front of me and pulled out a pen.

"What's this guy's name?"

"Jake Carter. He and his wife just bought a place off the Parkway in Belle Haven. You know the area?"

"Sure. High-rent district."

Track glanced out the window and nibbled a finger-nail.

"So, tell me something," I said. "Whose idea was it for you to buy the policy?"

"Oh, I don't know, probably his. You don't want a stranger holding an insurance policy on your life. Tends to decrease your life expectancy."

"Human nature being what it is."

"Exactly."

"Okay," I said, looking out the window again. "And now, when this guy dies, you're five hundred thousand dollars richer?"

"Something like that," Track said, sounding as if this type of thing happened every day.

"How old is this Carter guy?"

"He's a little more than sixty."

That startled me.

"You sold a 60-year-old man a half-million-dollar life insurance policy?"

"Of course not," he said, sounding indignant.

"How old was he when he bought it?"

"He was still in his fifties, probably."

I let that settle.

"Then you got a letter from the Bureau of Insur-ance?"

"Yeah."

"Can I see it?"

"I can send it to you," he said.

Track scratched at the scar under his beard.

"I want to make sure you know the whole story."

"I'm sure you do," I said, "but I'm not sure what you want me to do."

"I want you to make it go away, like Riley said you would."

"What's that mean? You want the bureau to approve the change in ownership of the policy?"

"The policy is mine," he said. "I just told you that."

Track's temper started to flare. The shaking of his leg increased, and he had gone back to rubbing his thumbs together.

"I'm worried about my license."

"Is that because of a threat you got from the bureau?"

"Seems to be. Can you fix it?"

"That sounds like a tall order."

"Riley says you're the guy for it."

"Did Riley tell you how much I charge?"

"Reasonable rates, he said."

"Reasonable rates mean it's still expensive."

"I figured that," he said. "I can pay you out of the money we recover."

I chuckled, shook my head, and watched him scowl in response to my skepticism. I was almost waiting for him to tell me I could benefit from the experience.

"I don't think we can work it that way," I said. "My industry is regulated, too."

He glanced around my office, noting the diplomas and my law license, framed in off-the-shelf metal. The only photograph in the room was of Marblehead Light, a landmark for lost mariners for centuries near my hometown. A framed sketch of the House of the Seven Gables filled the space above the credenza. The walls were otherwise bare, and the furniture was tired. I wasn't in business to impress anyone.

"I'll give you a tenth of the policy."

Track thought his offer would settle it. In a way, it did.

"I'm going to need a $5,000 retainer."

In a flash, I saw the face of the hard-hitting defenseman from years ago, ready to level an advancing midfielder.

"Let me think about it," he said.

I knew we were done for the moment, and as I got up so did Track. He pivoted toward the door, quickly shifting his weight with a smoothness that belied his girth and brought to mind a vivid image of him from an alumni game a year or two after my graduation. He had laid out a buddy of mine with a wicked body check, resulting in several of us spending hours in the radiology waiting room at the university hospital instead of enjoying ourselves on what should have been a team-building lark.

Track had a habit of leaving people injured in his wake.

As the door shut behind him, I wished I'd asked him for a lot more than five grand.

***

I decided to wait until the next morning to call Riley.

"Did you call to thank me or to complain?"

"Riley, when have I ever called you and not complained?"

"There was Brooke, that girl who . . ."

"Never mind that now."

"Well, I think I sent you a good one this time."

I had lost some sleep the night before. I needed the business, to be sure, but it wasn't a matter of paying the rent.

"What made you think that?" I said.

"It's a regulatory problem and the facts aren't in dispute. Track needs a fixer."

"All right, so he bought a viatical settlement. That's a big no-no with the bureau, but I assume if he cancels the deal the problem goes away with a slap on the wrist?"

"You disappoint me, Joth. Come on, if it was that easy, why would I have told him to call you?"

"I suppose Carter doesn't want to cancel the deal."

"He didn't tell you, did he?"

I heard Riley sigh.

"I told him to tell you."

"Come on, Riley. I'm waiting."

"He syndicated it."

I took in a lungful of air.

"He sold shares in it?"

"Well, to at least one person."

I could have kicked myself.

"What are the premiums on a five hundred-thou-sand-dollar policy on the life of a 60-year-old man?" I said.

"Probably pretty steep," said Riley, "but Track can afford it. He does pretty well."

"Who did he syndicate it to?"

"I don't know. One of his customers, I guess."

"So, they'll share the policy proceeds if this guy Carter dies?"

"When he dies, yeah. He's in his sixties and he smokes."

I thought again of the vicious hit Track had laid on my friend with the brutal efficiency of a farmer drowning a blind kitten.

"Yeah, who knows? That might be soon, and it changes things," I said. "Does the bureau know about the syndication?"

"I don't know."

"You sure, Riley?"

"I'm sure our friend didn't tell them," he said.

"Yeah? Well, somebody told the bureau something. Otherwise, there wouldn't be a letter, which by the way, I still haven't seen."

"Track Racker doesn't tell anybody any more than he has to," said Riley. "That's another reason I sent him to you."

"Okay, thanks for the referral."

I started to hang up, then thought of something else.

"And Riley, one more thing. Don't tell people I charge reasonable rates."

Chapter Two

The Man from Downstate

DP Tran owned a pre-World War II, yellow brick blockhouse on Wilson Boulevard, where he ran TwinKilling Investigations and TwinKilling Bailbonds from a spacious second floor office. The detective agency was on sabatical because DP's license had been revoked, but the sign still hung on the door. The first floor was divided into small offices suitable for solo law practices. I operated Jonathan Proctor & Associates, PC from one of these, although my firm had no associates and wasn't likely to need any in the near future.

DP was a small, lithe Vietnamese immigrant with a shaved head. Though he'd been born overseas, he had immigrated with his parents as an infant. Consequently, he spoke English as well as anyone who's been through 12 years of the Arlington public school system, except that when perturbed, he could swear like a man raised among families of longshoremen.

When I let myself into my office around ten the next morning, he was sitting in one of the two client chairs across from my desk.

"I thought I locked up last night," I said.

I sneered, making sure he could feel an edge in my annoyance.

Tran held up his passkey.

"I didn't think you'd mind."

"You know I do."

"But this is about business."

"What kind of business?"

DP scowled.

"Fucking Mitch is behind on his rent again."

I swung around behind my desk and dropped into the well-worn leather chair behind it.

"Maybe you better hire a lawyer."

"I just want you to talk to him."

I rolled my eyes.

Mitch Tressler, my co-tenant, was a trust and estates and real estate lawyer with a casual attitude toward his rent and almost everything else.

"Look, I've told you this before. He knows all the dodges, all the delaying tactics. Send him the five-day Pay-Or-Quit notice. He'll pay up before the interest kicks in."

"I'm not gonna do this every month. You tell him that."

My landlord had a carefully cultivated reputation as a martial arts master. The details were a little hazy, but I knew he was a non-confrontational man.

"That's what you get for letting him draft the lease."

"I'm tired of his horseshit," Tran whined. "Will you do this for me?"

"I will if you stop coming into my office uninvited."

"All right, it's a deal."

It wasn't much of a compromise, but I needed to talk to Mitch anyway.

I was rarely in the office before ten in the morning, but I was an early riser compared to Mitch. He had to pass my office to get to his, and as he strolled by about an hour later, I called his name and asked for a minute of his time.

Mitch looked like he'd slept in his clothes. In fact, I think he sometimes did. He defended his slothful appearance by explaining that he rarely met with clients, which was true enough, but it may also have explained why at age fifty-five he was practicing law out of a tiny, one-room office on skid row.

He stepped in and looked around warily.

"Mitch, you know what day of the month it is."

"Don't get cute with me, Joth."

"You can either deal with me or the Kung Fu master."

Mitch was a sizeable man, but he was as flabby as Track was solid. He made a disgusted sound, as if the whole matter offended him.

"Kung Fu, my ass. I been checking around. That Chink teaches T'ai Chi to old ladies and kooks at a retirement community."

"He's Vietnamese."

"Vietnamese, Chinese; he's a homophobe is what he is."

"Is he?"

Mitch hiked up his pants with a great show of dignity.

"Not that it matters to me personally," he said.

"No, of course not. Can I tell him you'll pay the rent today? It would make it a lot easier for all of us."

"I'll see what I can do."

Coming from Mitch, that was a firm commitment. I knew that if he paid, I'd get some credit with DP and that never hurt.

"While I've got you here, Mitch, what do you know about viaticals?"

His puffy face brightened, and he sat down in one of the two client chairs.

"Is this time billable?"

"It might be."

Mitch raised a tired eyebrow.

"If I land the client."

He thought about that and tossed his head, as if to get a final cobweb cleared.

"Okay, what do you want to know?"

"Let's say a financial planner buys back a policy on his client's life. What's the bureau of insurance likely to do?"

Mitch appeared disappointed in the simplicity of the inquiry.

"I suppose they'd make him divest."

"Anything else?"

He shrugged.

"A letter of reprimand, maybe. Viaticals aren't illegal in Virginia."

"What if he syndicated it to one of his other clients?"

As soon as I said this, his face lit up. Mitch was the sort of man who reveled in the difficulties of others. It made him feel better about himself.

"Then he's got a problem, Joth. Other people involved; fiduciary duty, you know the routine."

He turned up his beefy palms and grinned, sensing that somebody was soon to be in a world of hurt.

"That's embarrassing to the bureau. The bureau doesn't like to be embarrassed."

I nodded.

"Who does? Are we talking about a suspension?"

"At least."

He saw that he'd answered my question, and as he got up to leave, he continued.

"Who do I bill this time to?"

"Write it down. It's billable. Assuming you pay the rent today."

"Tomorrow."

"Tomorrow, then."

Mitch turned with a stiff nod, as if I'd agreed to terms for a duel.

"By the way Mitch, what's the spot on the Wizards game tonight?"

"Celtics giving two," he said, without missing a beat.

As I watched him leave, I wondered which side of that bet he had. DP's rent money was likely riding on the result of a basketball game.

***

A week later, Track appeared at my office unannounced. I hadn't forgotten about him. I'd been vacillating between disappointment over losing the fee he might've paid and a sense of relief over losing a client who made my skin crawl.

I invited him in, and he sat in the same UVA captain's chair as on his previous visit, where he looked out the window at the fog drifting up Wilson Boulevard. With a decisive gesture, he reached into his Harris Tweed sport coat and pulled out a roll of bills bound by a red elastic band. He removed the elastic with the panache of a man used to dealing in cash and spread forty crisp portraits of US Grant across the top of my desk.

"Two thousand now, Joth. I can bring you the balance in a week."

I took a good look at the money.

"Last week you offered me a fifty-thousand-dollar contingency. Now, you can't come up with a five-thousand-dollar retainer?"

"I'm cash poor at the moment. You know how it is."

I shrugged.

"It's a common problem," I said.

"What's your rate?"

I lied a little.

"$275 an hour."

"I'll pay you $300 an hour. But I can't come up with the big retainer right away."

"At $300 an hour, it can add up."

"Yeah, I talked to Riley. I understand how it works."

"I'm a better businessman than Riley."

"Everyone's a better businessman than Riley."

I took the money.

"You got the letter?"

Track took it from his inside coat pocket and slid it across the desk. It had been crumpled, as if someone had impulsively balled it up and thrown it in the trash before trying to flatten out the resulting creases and folds. There wasn't much in it: a statement of the complaint and a request that Track promptly respond. It was signed by Phillip Knott, Senior Administrator.

I got out a legal pad and took some notes.

"How'd the Bureau of Insurance find out about this problem?

"Dammed if I know, Joth. The government's got their hand in everywhere these days. You know that."

"You know anything about this Phillip Knott?"

Track shrugged.

"I Googled him. Bureaucrat. You know the type. Ex-military, but probably never advanced past lieutenant. The only thing he likes more than telling people what to do is being told what to do."

"You two ought to get along just fine."

I expected an angry glare. Instead, I got a laugh. I never liked Track's laugh, so full of the sounds of unearned superiority and condescension, but this one carried a note of sincerity.

"I guess. You know, I'm in sales."

He turned a hand over, as if to indicate his kinship with those who cooked up schemes for a living.

"No rules, just personality. But we're all in sales when you get right down to it. The only sure bet I know is that everyone's going to die. I'm really doing everyone a favor by taking it off his hands."

I took a moment to let that sink in.

"Who were Carter's beneficiaries? Before he transferred the policy, I mean."

"His wife and her kids from her first marriage. He never had kids of his own."

"How's his wife feel about it?

Track squirmed at this question. I'd touched a nerve.

"I'm sure she's fine with it."

"You talk to her?"

His eyes met mine, then flashed away.

"Yeah."

"What's her name?"

He hesitated.

"Juanita."

"Try again."

I could see him consider another lie. His beefy shoulders sagged, and he gave it up.

"Maureen, then."

"Uh-huh. So, instead of paying premiums until the guy dies, you took them over. Am I right?"

Track nodded and looked pained doing so.

"Plus," he said, "I paid him fifteen thousand up front."

I raised my eyebrows.

"He needed the cash."

"Does this explain why you're cash poor?"

"Look, Joth, I've got a lot of stuff going on," he said. He sounded more irritable than usual.

"Lot of deals, you know, lot of money moving around. You wouldn't understand. It's not your scene."

"I thought you said Carter won the lottery?"

"Yeah, but she controls the money. This gives him a little income of his own."

I looked again at the letter Track had brought. Knott's initial approach was by the book: identify the issue and demand an explanation.

"Nothing in here about you getting out of the viatical."

"I suppose that's coming. Even though it's legal in Virginia. Right now, Knott just wants to make sure nobody gets hurt."

"Who might get hurt?"

"Bad choice of words, Joth. Look, this guy is just a paper pusher with regulations to enforce."

"How 'bout Carter's wife's kids? Don't they get hurt?"

"They got no stake in it at all," he said indignantly. "Not anymore."

"How about the person you sold part of the policy to?"

Track's head popped up, and he met my eyes for a moment; something he seldom did, as if he'd been trained to do anything but look a person square in the eye.

"Yeah, I sold an interest to a customer. Alice Moriarty. She needed a small investment vehicle, so I killed two birds with one stone."

I held up the letter.

"Have you talked to her about this?"

"No."

"Why not?"

"Look, it's an expensive policy. I'm not made of money, Joth. I needed help carrying the premiums, so I sold her an interest."

"How much of an interest?"

He hesitated.

"And I want the truth, Track. It's the only way."

He ignored use of the nickname this time. Events had overtaken his need for propriety. "Ten percent. She's protected, so that should be the end of it."

"You paid Carter a cash amount, plus you're paying the premiums; is that right?"

"Yeah."

"And the policy was formally transferred to you?"

He nodded.

"How much did you say the premiums are?"

"I don't know."

"And how much of the premiums is Moriarty paying you?"

"I'd have to check."

Track had been a bull on the lacrosse field, but he slid around the truth like a shifty attackman dodging toward the goal.

"But she's entitled to ten percent of the proceeds of the policy when Carter dies?"

"That's right. It's a sweet deal for her."

I shot him a look of disgust and let it register before I continued.

"So, this customer of yours, this Moriarty, she's defraying the monthly premiums by making a payment to you every month?"

"Yup."

"Okay. I'm going to make a call to the guy from the bureau and see what I can do. But first, I need to see the policy and the assignment of it to you."

"No problem."

"And your contract with Moriarty?"

His eyes drifted to the window.

"I'll see what I can do."

***

A few days later, I got the insurance policy and the Declaration of Beneficiaries in the mail, with no cover letter or explanation. The policy premiums were steeper than I thought. That part of it was in order, but the sole assignee of the benefits was Frank Racker. No mention of an Alice Moriarty or any other co-beneficiary and Track's package did not include a contract between him and Moriarty.

I gave it a few days, then called and asked him about it. By now I recognized his pattern of obfuscation, and I cut him off before he could get started.

"You don't have a contract, do you?"

"I've got it someplace, Joth. Just can't lay my hands on it at the moment."

"If you don't have one, it might explain why Phil Knott got involved."

I heard Track curse under his breath.

"That old bag."

As we hung up, Track said Phillip Knott would be glad to talk to me. He was right. I emailed to set up a call and Knott got right back to me.

"Do you have time next week for lunch?" he asked after we exchanged introductions and pleasantries.

"Lunch? I'm a long way from Richmond."

"That's all right."

He had a little hint of that overstated First Family of Virginia drawl. You don't hear that too much anymore; there aren't too many of those first families left, and it occurred to me that I might have found some common ground. Track claimed to have Alexandria roots that ran back to the Revolution, and I made a mental note to gather some useful details.

"I get up in your neck of the woods a lot. Northern Virginia is my beat. These things always go better face to face."

I was apprehensive but agreed. He paused, and I heard his chair squeak as if he were leaning forward to consult a calendar.

"How 'bout next Tuesday?"

"Next Tuesday's fine."

"You know the Shirlington?"

"The Shirlington Grand?"

"That's the place."

"That's a little rich for my budget, Mr. Knott."

"Don't worry, we can expense it. See you there at one o'clock? That's my usual lunch hour."

He seemed insistent, and I wanted every edge I could get.

"Sure, thanks. You want me to make a reservation?"

"No, I'll take care of it."

"How am I going to recognize you?"

"I'm usually the best dressed guy in the place."

"Don't worry, I won't provide any competition."

***

After hanging up, I called Track to report on my progress.

"Don't trust anything that bastard says."

"Bastard? I didn't think you knew him."

"I don't, but he works for the government, and they're all vipers. He fits the mold to a T."

Anybody who got in Track's way was a bastard by definition.

"It might be that you have something in common," I said. "He sounds like Old Virginia."

"Nobody's more Old Virginia than me."

"I know. Can you give me a little background, something I can use to try to create . . ."

"I'm a direct descendant of a Confederate general," Track said. "How's that?"

He then launched into the story of Montgomery Corse, the Alexandria native who commanded a brigade under Longstreet. I stopped him at the first opportunity.

"Impressive. And it can't hurt."

"Anything else?"

"Yeah, I want Moriarty's contract."

Track hung up without a word.

Track's reluctance to deal with the contract was not reassuring, but I knew the missing document would eventually surface—if it existed. Meanwhile, I had to prepare myself for this well-dressed government viper.

***

I consider the habit of punctuality as just good manners. It's also smart when your client is accused of misconduct. With these two principles in mind, I made my way to the Shirlington Grand.

I walked in at ten of one and sat at the bar. I ordered a Coke and kept an eye on the door. The bar was empty and the bartender, a twenty-something female in black pants and a white button-down, was bored.

"Waiting for somebody?"

She spoke into the mirror as she polished the glassware.

"Yes. Business meeting."

"Must be nice."

"Just another day."

She chuckled. She was tall and thin with tired highlights in her mousy brown hair.

"I need to get into that kind of business."

"I'm with a government agency. You wouldn't like it."

"Better than being on your feet all day."

I took a sip and turned again toward the door.

"Looks like a slow lunch hour."

"Yeah, spring weather."

"I understand it gets busy here in the late afternoon."

She looked me over in the mirror, noting my tired tweed jacket and knit tie.

"I just work here, man. I don't control who comes in."

It was an odd reply, and I filed it away.

Knott strutted in promptly at one. I recognized him by his haberdashery: slim cut European suit and a crisp white shirt adorned with gold cufflinks. He looked around and picked me out as I slid off the barstool. Track had described him as ex-military, but I wasn't prepared for this bantam rooster. He looked to be about my age, with a thick head of close-cropped blond hair, blue eyes, and the disarming smile of a rush chairman.

"Hey Darla," he said, and the barmaid nodded at him.

"You've been here before," I said.

He granted me an ingratiating smile and gestured toward Darla.

"This place is very civilized. Shall we go upstairs?"

Upstairs we found a booth and settled in. He ordered an Arnold Palmer while I studied the menu.

"If you like fish," he said, "try the trout."

I don't much like trout, but I took his advice.

"Your family been in Virginia long?" I asked.

He nodded as if I'd complimented him.

"Yes sir. Since Jamestown."

"Ah, then you and Frank have something in common."

The little man's eyes brightened inquisitively, and I regaled him with the family history I had learned from Track.

"Oh yes. His great-great grandfather commanded a brigade under Longstreet."

"I didn't know that."

Knott nodded his head thoughtfully.

"And now they want to change the names of schools and roads," he said.

"Revisionist history. Or so Frank holds."

"Indeed. And your family?"

"Well, I've got northern roots myself."

"I see."

"Not to fear," I said, trying not to wink. "I went to college here. UVA. Got an education in more ways than one."

"Well then, I'll take this up with Frank next time I see him."

"I'm sure you'll have a lot to agree on."

He smiled as if he'd said too much. I folded my hands and waited.

"I'm glad he hired you. Always better when they have a lawyer involved. Then it's all just business."

"He's taking it pretty seriously."

"These are difficult matters."

Knott studied the light fixture above us.

"When a man's livelihood is called into question, I find that meeting in a social setting helps to break the ice. It allows for a more cordial discussion."

"I don't think there's really much of a controversy," I said, adopting a casually positive tone.

"How much do you know about viaticals?"

"I know they're legal in Virginia."

He peeked at his neatly manicured nails.

"Sure."

Then he put his elbows on the table and steepled his fingers.

"Viatical. It comes from the Latin word *viaticum*, referring to the Last Rites of the Catholic Church."

"If I ever knew that, I'd forgotten."

"Ex-altar boy?"

"Hardly."

"Well, as you said, they're legal in Virginia, unlike many states. It seems counterintuitive, doesn't it? When someone holds an insurance policy on another man's life, you'd expect his life expectancy to dip pretty quick."

"That's what came to my mind."

"The Supreme Court has held that a life insurance policy is personal property and should be treated that way. People can do what they want with their personal property, subject to reasonable public policy controls, of course. If I have a valuable asset, I ought to be able to sell it, don't you think?"

I nodded.

"Let the seller beware," I said.

The food came. He had ordered soft shell crabs, and he tested one with the back of the tines of his fork, then looked around impatiently for the waiter. The response was prompt. He pointed with his chin.

"These are overdone."

"I'm sorry sir, I'll take them back."

"Never mind now," he said crossly. "I'm in a rush."

The waiter apologized again and slinked away from the table.

Knott recovered his equipoise quickly.

"You know what made it an issue? The AIDS crisis in the 80s and 90s. Many men needed money for catastrophic medical bills. Many of them didn't have wives or children, the traditional beneficiaries of financial planning. These life insurance policies became a lifesaver—literally, in many cases. You could turn them into money to pay for desperately needed medical treatments. In its wisdom, the Virginia legislature approved."

"You seem to have sympathy for someone in Frank's position."

"I don't know what Mr. Carter's particular needs are. That's not my job."

He tossed a hand, as if he were anointing one of his subjects.

"We, the Commonwealth, we just don't want anyone to get hurt."

This was the same concern Track had voiced and I guessed it was the standard line from a continuing education seminar.

"Fortunately, I don't think anyone will," I said.

I detected a twinkle in his eye.

"Except Mrs. Moriarty."

I wondered if this was why he wanted to meet in person—to see how I'd react to this tidbit of information.

"She's protected," I said.

"Is she?"

He poked at his crabs as if he feared infection.

"What I like about your client, Jon—can I call you Jon?"

"I go by Joth."

Knott nodded, processing the name like a piece of data.

"Joth. That's an unusual name."

"Not in my family."

"Well, what I like about him, Joth, is that he tells the truth. What I don't like about him is that he never tells *all* of the truth."

I knew we were talking about the same guy.

"He could flip the policy to someone else and get Mrs. Moriarty out of the middle."

Knott stroked his chin.

"Could. Have to be somebody for whom it makes financial sense. Your client's got an ethical duty to her, you know."

"He's well aware of that."

Knott dropped his chin into the palm of his hand and studied me.

"You're aware, of course, that Mrs. Moriarty is older than Mr. Carter?"

I didn't know that, but I pushed on as if I did.

"Your real concern is Mrs. Moriarty," I said. "That she's protected."

"You think fast, Joth. But she's not protected."

"And how might she be protected?"

"She wants her money back."

"I see. Or perhaps he could give her what he promised her?"

"Which is?"

"She called you because Racker hadn't given her a formal assignment, and she got nervous. Is that right?"

He smiled.

"Can't blame her at her age."

I nodded politely.

"Then can we settle the case along those lines?"

"I'd prefer he take her out of the policy. Of course, if that's not possible, we might be able to work it another way."

"You'll accept a formal assignment if he can't buy it back?"

"I didn't say that. I'll say possibly. If things fall into place." Knott raised his napkin from his lap and carefully patted his lips and continued. "Although you know we have to keep the skids of the system greased."

I tried not to react, but he was watching me closely.

"I think it's fair to say that my client's concern is keeping his insurance license."

"I think it's fair to say that this can be arranged. Separately."

Knott raised an eyebrow.

"You mentioned you were buying lunch," he said.

I knew exactly what he was asking me to buy, and it wasn't just lunch. I changed my posture and made sure he noticed.

"You said you want to make sure no one gets hurt," I said. "How do you do that?"

"Oversight," he said, with an academic flourish. "It takes a lot of time and effort."

He took out a business card, turned it over and wrote a number on the back.

"This is the best way to reach me."

I turned the card over.

"Can I use this email?"

"I'm an oral guy, Mr. Proctor. I prefer to deal on the phone."

As the waiter was processing my credit card, I glanced at my watch.

"I'm sure you want to beat rush hour back to Richmond."

"Oh, I've got some time. I'll just sit in the bar and check my emails."

He stood up, and so did I. He held out his hand, and I shook it with all the grace and southern charm I could muster.

***

I called Track from my car, figuring it would be a short conversation.

"How old is Mrs. Moriarty?"

He reacted like I'd asked him the age of his sister's dog.

"Oh, I don't know, Joth. Older than me."

"Yeah? Do you really think she needs a life insurance policy on someone younger than her?"

"He's a guy. She's a woman. She'll outlive him by years."

"Sure," I said. "Look, Knott wants you to buy the policy back from her. Take her out of it."

"The policy?"

"What else are we talking about?"

"That's all? That would surprise me."

"That's what the man said."

"Can't do it."

"It would solve all your problems."

Track took a second to respond.

"You don't know Knott."

"What do you mean 'you can't do it?' "

"It means I won't. I haven't got the cash."

"Well, then, get it."

"If I had the cash, I wouldn't need you, Joth. You're going to have to think of something else. Besides, I don't trust Knott."

Neither did I, but I didn't tell that to Track.

Chapter Three

Lottery Winner

Track's comments about Jake Carter and his wife piqued my curiosity. A web search provided a few clues. Carter was Ivy League educated and came from a Virginia family with roots that rivaled those which Track claimed for himself. On the other hand, his spotty employment history and reputation as a social gadfly suggested a dilettante.

Track was right about the wife: her maiden name evoked glittering jewelry, polo ponies, and country estates. Considering the substantial difference in age, I wondered if their partnership was a late-in-life alliance between money and the one thing money couldn't buy: pedigree.

I was still sure that Track was not telling me everything.

***

For a man of leisure, Jake Carter was awfully hard to pin down. After several days of fruitless efforts to reach him at home, I showed up one day late in the morning at his sprawling home just off the George Washington Parkway on the banks of the Potomac. It was built of red brick with white columns out front, but it lacked the authenticity of the antebellum South that the builder seemingly had tried so hard to evoke. Contrary to the classical style, Carter's house was asymmetrical. The windows were out of proportion and lacked shutters, and a three-car garage had been tacked on to one side.

Mr. Jefferson would not have approved. Overall, it instilled the uncomfortable sense of a builder who had tried to include all the modern amenities within a style that wouldn't accommodate them. As I took this all in, a woman I knew to be his wife from her photos on the web suddenly appeared at the door. She was not unattractive, but big-boned and substantial, and her expression called to mind an underfed watchdog.

"Try the marina," she said, turning away.

"What marina?"

"Where he keeps his boat," she said.

With that, she quickly shut the door.

A decal on the back bumper of a Land Rover in the driveway provided a clue, and a few minutes later, I pulled into the Washington Sailing Marina on Daingerfield Island.

Back in George Washington's day, Daingerfield may have been an island, but it was now a 106-acre, federally owned spit of land jutting into the Potomac, just east of the Parkway. The marina was built into a cove tucked between the northern point and the parkland that comprised the shoreline. The compound featured a four-star restaurant, a snack bar, and a chandlery, where the college kid behind the counter smiled at the mention of Carter's name and pointed me to F dock.

There were probably twenty boats tied bow-in to the slips along each side of the dock; modest sloops of twenty-five feet or less, fitted together like teeth. Access to the dock was restricted by a heavy metal gate at the top of the gangplank that wouldn't give when I rattled it. Looking through the bars, I saw a portly gentleman in Bermuda shorts and a white T-shirt puttering about a boat, halfway down on the right.

"Jake Carter!"

His head swung around at the name.

"Jake Carter! A minute of your time, please."

He considered for a moment, then ambled up toward the gangplank, studying me as he wiped his hands on the ratty tail of a T-shirt bearing the logo of an Old Town bar.

"What can I do for you, Captain?"

"I'm a friend of Frank's. Frank Racker."

44

He took an imitation corncob pipe out his mouth, nodded slightly and waited for me to continue.

"He's in a little bit of hot water over the insurance policy he sold you."

Jake laughed briefly, as if he were truly amused, and then he shook his head.

"Which one?"

"The one he bought back."

"I told him. That guy doesn't listen to anybody."

He nodded at me, about to move away, as if he were finished.

"That's a Seaward Sloop, isn't it?" I said.

Jake stared at me for a moment, then turned and studied his vessel.

"Sure is."

"What's it draw?"

"Four-and-a-half, with the centerboard down."

"The Potomac's shallower than that in a lot of places."

"Yeah, once you get out of the channel."

His eyes narrowed, checking me more carefully.

"Well, no sense in talking from here."

As he walked up to the top of the gangplank, Jake reached into his pocket and removed a nautical key ring with a plastic fob hanging on it. He waved it in front of the lock box. I heard a metallic click, and he pulled the gate open.

"Pretty nice system to keep the riff-raff out," I said.

Jake chuckled.

"Except my wife has the other fob."

I followed him down toward the boat.

When spring comes to Virginia, summer is not far behind. It was in the mid-60s and the sun was bright in a cloudless blue sky.

"You aren't from this state, are you?" he said, looking me over as we walked together down the dock.

"No."

"Yankee accent," he said.

I detected a tone of mock indignation.

"I'm still working hard to lose it."

"You say you're Frank's friend. You a reenactor?'

"Excuse me?"

He turned to measure my expression.

"Frank and I are Civil War reenactors. I guess you didn't know that."

His eyes twinkled, and he looked me over more carefully.

"I'm guessing you're his lawyer?"

"Does he need one?"

"People like Frank always need lawyers, don't they?"

"Why is that, Mr. Carter?"

He smirked and paused to study my expression. Neither of us wanted to give up the first pawn.

"You say you're his friend?"

"Not exactly."

Jake nodded, as if he understood the limits my answer implied.

"He doesn't have a lot of friends."

"Yeah, and Frank says you're one of them."

"I don't have a lot of friends either. Even my wife would rather have me down here than under foot in the house, but that's a good thing. We're both cantankerous coots, Frank and me."

Jake stopped and stood with his hands on his hips, squinting up at the masthead of his little sloop. She was rigged for solo sailing, with a self-furling jib wrapped around the forestay and the halyards and sheets ran into the cockpit. The fiberglass hull was deep red with white trim and it looked newly painted. Glancing around, I quickly assessed it as one of the best fitted and maintained vessels on F Dock. I made sure that Jake noticed my admiration.

"Looks brand new."

He sucked unproductively on the pipe, took it out and examined the bowl.

"It's not. Bought it used. The slip's worth more than the boat. Ought to look new, though. I spend more time working on it than I spend sailing it."

"Up and down the river gets boring."

"Can't remember the last time I took her out, to tell you the truth. Some men have a club, I've got the boat. But you came to talk about the viatical."

"I did," I said, feeling almost sheepish for a moment.

"Well, come on aboard. I'll tell you over a beer."

His extended hand conveyed a genuine invitation. I hopped aboard and waited as Jake gingerly made his way over the gunwale. Then I held out my hand.

"Joth Proctor."

He took it smoothly in the kind of soft, fleshy paw that I didn't associate with the rigors of sailing.

"Jake. That's what everyone calls me, except my wife."

"What does she call you?"

"She calls me lazy," he said, with a smile at his well-practiced witticism.

Though the day was bright and sunny, it was still early in the season, and the boats berthed along the dock rocked quietly. Carter's boat was called *Southern Patriot*. It featured a newly stained mahogany tiller, and the banquettes along either side of the cockpit were unpadded. The white fiberglass gleamed in the morning sun. He stepped down into the cabin and emerged with a pair of flotation cushions and two Molsens. He opened one with a jackknife bottle opener and handed it to me, and as I sat on one of the cushions with the sun behind me I counted three empty green bottles in a bucket in the cockpit. He'd also retrieved a pouch of tobacco, and I took the opportunity to study him as he painstakingly refilled his pipe.

Carter was an unremarkable man. He had the paunch and thinning hair I'd have expected of a man of his generation. His features were soft and fair. He hadn't shaved in a day and had the doe-like eyes of an untroubled man.

"You a boat owner yourself?" he said.

It seemed awfully early for a beer, but it was ice cold, and the day was warm.

"No," I said, "been around them a little. I know enough to keep myself out of trouble."

"Well, that's what's it's all about, isn't it?"

Jake's eyes ran up the mast, fastened on the north pointing wind arrow at the peak. He then looked halfway toward me.

"That what Frank has?" he said. "Trouble?"

"The guy from the state doesn't seem too exercised about it."

"That would be Phillip Knott?"

"You pay attention, Jake."

He relit the pipe and looked at me through a series of vigorous pulls.

"You talked to him?"

"Took me out to lunch."

Jake's eyes brightened, and he laughed.

"Take you to the Shirlington?"

"Matter of fact he did," I said, sharing the chuckle.

"The Shirlington!"

Jake's eyebrows bobbed lasciviously.

"Now what do you suppose that's all about?"

"Maybe he just wanted to get out of Richmond."

"I'll bet he's got a girl up here."

"Maybe. By the way, how long ago did Frank sell you the policy?"

Jake examined the bowl of the pipe, and then his eyes traveled to the main halyard, as if checking it for frays.

"What did Frank tell you?"

"You know Frank. As little as possible."

"Am I at any risk here?"

It was a fair question and a smart one to ask.

"I don't see how. He sold you a life insurance policy. That's what he does for a living. You're entitled to sell it to anybody you want."

"Who owns the policy right now?"

I paused and thought it through.

"He paid you fifteen thousand dollars . . ."

"Twelve, and he hasn't paid it yet."

"He gave you a note?"

"Frank deals in cash. If you were Frank's friend, you'd know that."

He took a pull on his pipe.

I cleared my throat.

"You mean you signed the policy over to him before he finished paying you?"

"Of course."

"He just changed the beneficiary and took over the payments?"

Jake tried not to look chagrined.

"That's how he said we should do it. He's my financial advisor, after all."

"There might have been a better way."

"And that would be?"

I started to shrug and thought better of it.

"Well, he's my client and you're not, but most people like to see the money before they sign something over."

"So, who owns the policy?"

I took a long sip of the beer.

"I'd say the owner of the policy is whoever the insurance company shows on its books. Not to say you couldn't challenge that. Depends on your deal."

"That son of a fox."

"When's the final payment?"

"Well, it was twenty-four months. Do the math. Next year."

"Don't you have a written contract?"

"That's another thing Frank doesn't deal in."

I waited for him to catch my eye, feeling sympathy for this hint of remorse.

"How far behind is he in the payments?"

"A month or two. I bitch, but I know he's good for it."

"What makes you think that?"

Jake's eyes climbed the mast again and rested where the crosstrees glinted in the morning sun.

"Frank's a man of faith, you know. Very devoted."

"Did he tell you that?"

"Didn't have to. You can see it in the way he carries himself."

I kept me eyebrows right where they belonged and said nothing.

I don't trust what people say about their religious beliefs because those kinds of statements are always self-serving. Instead, I watch how they behave. The disparity is often instructive.

"Frank says you don't need the money."

Jake laughed heartily.

"If I'm dead, I'm not getting the money. It's my wife who doesn't need the money. That's why I sold it back. One thing I'm good at is burning through money. I needed the cash for this boat."

A wave of his hand encompassed his domain.

"My wife's sure as hell not supporting this."

"Whose idea was it?"

"To sell it back, you mean? I think it was Frank's, now that you mention it."

"Does Frank need the money?"

Jake laughed.

"Frank needs the thrill. He's a . . . what do you call it? Adrenaline junkie? He likes the high wire. If it wasn't against the rules, he probably wouldn't have done it."

I smiled and nodded.

"You're an insightful man," I said.

I finished the beer and placed the empty bottle in the drink caddy that hung on the stern rail.

"Reenactor. What did you mean by that, Jake?"

"That's how I got to know your friend."

"Client," I said.

"I thought you might be one, too. You got the look, you know. Lean, kind of chiseled. Like you're ready to lead your regiment up Cemetery Ridge."

"Cemetery Ridge. Gettysburg?"

"That's right," he said, puffing up his chest with pride.

I had an ancestor on that ridge that day, but he was on the other side of the stone wall. I'm sure my expression revealed my bafflement, but he didn't appear surprised or annoyed by my uncomfortable reaction.

"The 28th Virginia, that's my regiment. We participate in the battle reenactments. You've probably read about us."

I had read about reenactors in the *Post* and in local magazines, and they'd always struck me as bizarre: grown-up men, most of them with families, decked out in fantastic costumes exorcising suppressed childhood desires.

"Frank does all that?"

"Oh, he does. Does it up right, too. Even got a horse."

I remembered what Track had told me.

"I understand he's descended from a general."

"That's right," Jake said, with growing enthusiasm. "Montgomery Corse. Led Pickett's Charge at Gettysburg."

"I didn't know that."

"I'm surprised. He's quite proud of it. We take authenticity pretty seriously."

"I imagine Frank takes it as seriously as anybody."

Jake puffed thoughtfully on his pipe.

"You should see how he gets up: gray flannel, lots of gold braid. Frank could be General Pickett himself in that get up, and no one would complain, but he's Monty Corse."

"Fascinating."

Jake looked closely at me for a sign of sarcasm, and I barely withstood his scrutiny.

"Come on out and watch us sometime. We never miss the Gettysburg fight. You'll get a real lesson in history."

"Maybe I will. For now, I've taken up enough of your time."

"Did you get what you were after?"

"I'm not sure what I was after, Jake. Just wanted to get acquainted."

Jake's face lit up with an amiable grin.

"Come by any time. I'm usually down here."

I smiled in return; it would have been hard not to.

"There are worse places to spend a day."

He took a pipe tool out of his pocket and tamped the bowl.

"Not many better."

As I made my way up the gangplank, I turned and got another glimpse at the red and white vessel tugging lightly at its docking lines. *Southern Patriot*, it read on the port side of the hull. I shook my head and chuckled at the thought of Track Racker riding a horse across the fields of Gettysburg, all tricked out in Confederate gray, like the opening scene of a late night docudrama on the History Channel.

Chapter Four

Riding Time

Dan Crowley considered me a regular at his Crystal City gentlemen's club, Riding Time. I had met him almost a decade before, when my visits to his establishment were purely social. I was struggling to recover from a bad breakup, and he did what he could to help. Before long, I was defending Dan's girls against the sort of trivial misdemeanor charges that seemed to be a cost of doing business in that industry.

Success bred success. When Irish Dan, as he had come to be known, had business for me, we met at his place. We both preferred it that way.

He had called my office, leaving the inartful message that one of his girls had got her "tit in a wringer."

Riding Time was jammed into a long, windowless room among a row of hangouts for government contractors and federal employees. The low ceiling held in the noise and the cigar smoke. I leaned forward to make myself heard over the pulsing backbeat. The girl behind the bar was new. I told her who I was and nursed a beer while I waited.

Dan runs a main stage and a cage fitted with a pole near a pool table in the back. Each girl's cycle went from the main stage to the cage to a half-hour break while the rest of the crew worked through their routines.

I didn't notice Jade in the cage, but a few minutes after my arrival, she pulled up the stool next to me. She had shimmering copper hair and yes, her eyes were green; eyes that always shouted to me that she didn't need to be sitting on a bar stool in a red silk robe over her scanty work clothes. Her skin was moist from her work; the ends of her long hair were matted, and she exuded a raw and compelling animal scent.

"Here on business with the boss?"

She was fishing.

"What makes you think that?"

She rolled her eyes.

"I never see you anymore. You must be pretty busy."

"Keeping the wolves away from the door."

"A couple of the girls wouldn't have driver's licenses if it weren't for you," she said, with a friendly nudge of her shoulder.

I told her I appreciated it. I also appreciated her dimpled smile, which was the cutest in the place.

"I wonder what Dan's got for you?"

"He didn't tell me."

"Good."

I glanced around for Dan while Jade made more conversation.

"You like what you do, Joth?"

"Yeah, I like it."

I liked the work. What I didn't like was the dehumanizing process of chasing after it, doing the social glad-handing that was the price of any real financial success in my business. Instead, I skipped that kind of thing and waited for the phone to ring.

"You do a lot of stuff for Dan, don't you?"

"I've got other clients. What makes you so nosy today?"

Then she asked me if I had a girlfriend, which wasn't really small talk.

I was spared a response when Dan appeared. He swatted Jade's butt and chased her down a stool.

"No way to treat a lady," I said firmly, but Dan was not a man to be concerned about political correctness.

"That ain't no lady," he replied with a cackle, as he took over her stool.

Dan had a florid map-of-Ireland face with a pair of wide blue eyes that seemed to chase troubles away like a shamrock.

"What's this about?"

He gestured with a shrug of his shoulder.

"It's about your girl, Jade."

She leaned forward intently as Dan unfolded a misdemeanor warrant for assault and battery and pushed it toward me. It listed Jennifer Tedesco as the defendant. It was a form designed to reveal minimum information: the date, place and time of the alleged offense, identifying information about the defendant, and the court date.

I leaned forward and looked past Dan at Jade, seeking her confirmation, and she nodded somberly.

"What happened?"

Dan answered the question.

"Oh, you know, he took a shine to her, asked her out, she said no, of course, or so she says, and then he offered her money."

Dan looked probingly at Jade.

"And she kicked him."

"Kicked him in the nuts," she said sharply and without apology.

"Did some real damage with those pointy shoes she wears, if you can believe what's on the warrant. The guy lost a testicle."

"And he told this to the Commonwealth?" I said.

"Without the proposition, of course."

Dan prodded her.

"Is that how it happened, Jade?"

She nodded with conviction.

"Maybe I ought to hear what Jade has to say."

I bobbed my eyebrows for emphasis.

"Just the two of us?"

That was his expectation.

"Whatever you say."

Dan nodded and got up.

"Do what you do. Fix it and send me the bill."

Jade and I took a booth in the back and sat across from each other. She wasn't scared. It would take a lot more than a misdemeanor warrant to shake Jade, but she was apprehensive. Her green eyes were large, round and curious.

"You disagree with anything Dan said?"

"No, he told it like it happened, like I told Dan in the first place."

I shot her a frown.

"You know whatever you tell me goes no further, Jade. Your friends here will tell you that."

"I know."

She scratched her shoulder with her chin, avoiding my eyes.

"I told you, it was just like I told Dan."

"I see. So, who is this guy?"

I looked at the warrant.

"This Chris Barkley."

Jade batted her eyes, seemingly surprised to hear that name spoken out loud.

"He's Mama's son."

"Who's Mama?"

She cocked her head like I was making a bad joke, and an image of a stern, heavy set woman came flooding back to me. Mama Barkley was Dan's partner. Or had been. It had been years since I'd heard that name. Mama's son was Chris. I tried to remember if I'd ever met him.

"You ever go out with him?"

She hesitated.

"A few times, yeah. We all have. That's what Dan says we have to do to in order keep the peace."

"The peace? What peace?"

"Keep Mama happy."

Mama, I thought. What, exactly, had happened to Mama? Had I once known about it and forgotten?

"Young guy?"

"No. A little over thirty, I guess. About your age."

I stifled a grin at her appealing naivety.

"Have you . . ." I said, opening my palms, ". . . uh, had any personal interaction with him?"

The question didn't faze her.

"You know, tips, small talk, stuff like that. He comes in here a lot. Dan tells us to be good to him."

"So, you bumped into him after work?"

"It was just a couple of days ago."

She tilted her head to confirm that date on the warrant.

"He was waiting for me when I got off. Scared the shit out of me to tell you the truth."

"And?"

"And he said a hundred dollars for a half hour of your time. And that's when I kicked him."

"Just like that?"

"Just like that."

"What does he say happened?"

"I don't know. This came as a big shock to me. I got arrested, you know."

"Have you ever been . . . has anybody ever said anything like that to you before?"

"Not since I been working for Dan, no."

Jade read my face and pouted.

"Look, I know I'm no saint, but what I do working here, I mean, well, it doesn't give a man the right to say something like that, you know?"

"Yeah, I do."

She looked at the clock.

"Look, I gotta go. My set's about to start, and I have to freshen up."

"Okay."

I stood up.

"Tell Dan I need to talk to him."

Dan sauntered over a few minutes later and slid into the booth. He scanned the room to make sure no one was watching, then grinned and shook his head.

"How 'bout that, huh? You never know what's gonna happen around here."

"Yeah, different adventure every day."

He chuckled appreciatively and winked.

"But always a comfortable place to spend an afternoon."

Familiar, certainly, though not truly comfortable; not unlike the prep school that held a place at the other end of my life's spectrum.

"You said you believe her. Is that true, Dan?"

He pinched his lower lip between his fingertips.

"I don't know. She's usually pretty straight with me, but I know she's got a bit of a temper."

I looked at the warrant again.

"Assault and battery. Must have been pretty mad about something."

"Well, I know he was pretty sweet on her."

"How do you know that?"

"Oh, I got four or five girls here who'll tell you that."

"I understand he's Mama's kid."

Dan scowled and narrowed his eyes.

"Didn't you buy her out?"

"No. She still owns half the stock."

"I haven't seen her around here . . ."

"She had a stroke five, six years ago. You remember. She's in a facility. Who do you think pays for that?"

"In a facility?"

"Jeez, Joth, you losin' your marbles? The stroke nearly killed her."

I pushed back from the table as I put it together.

"Chris Barkley. His mother's your partner, and she's in a facility. He's got her power of attorney?"

"The light finally comes on, counselor."

I placed my finger by my nose and considered the problem.

"Okay, Dan. Best-case scenario for Chris: he likes her; he happens to be passing by the place as she gets out. He says something innocent and she ruins him. That sound like it?"

"I think so."

"Big guy?"

"No, he's about Jade's height, and she's only five foot nine. Tell the truth, Joth, I don't know about this proposition part. I think she probably saw him and thought he was stalking her, and she overreacted. Why else would he go to the police? I mean, I've known him

65

since he was a kid. He always seemed to have good intentions."

"Sounds like it might be a case I'll have to try."

The thought of putting Jade and Dan's other girls on the stand didn't appeal to me. Dan didn't want that either, but he wouldn't let that concern deter him.

"Chris might not want that," said Dan.

"There might not be much choice. The Commonwealth's not going to dismiss it."

"Okay, now here's the kicker."

Dan grinned and pulled a cheap spiral-bound notebook from his shirt pocket. He put it in front of me and I opened it to the first page, then leafed through, occasionally glancing up at Dan with appreciation.

"Where'd you get this stuff?"

"Just keeping my ear to the ground, counselor."

"You don't miss much, do you?"

He chuckled, pleased with the effect he'd wrought.

"You just have to know where to look."

I shut the notebook.

"This ought to help," I said.

"It's ticklish, you know?"

"Is Mama okay?"

"She's barely conscious."

"Really? And the kid?"

"Look, he doesn't know how good he's got it. I pay all of his mom's medical bills, plus a little a something for him each month, you know? It's good for him, and it's good for me. I don't want to upset the apple cart."

I looked again at the warrant.

"Are you willing to have this tried?"

Dan chewed on my question.

"Chris was hurt. Embarrassed. Do what you gotta do."

I put my finger to my lips and looked away. Thinking back to my younger days, I could picture the elderly woman with the heavy arms who ran the bar and kept patrons in line, but it was Dan that I had got to know. It was Dan who hired me—small matters at first, nickel-and-dime stuff. Mama deferred to him on the day-to-day business matters and she was irrelevant to me. But Mama still owned half the stock.

"I thought you bought her out?"

Dan straightened up and looked at me.

"We had an understanding, Mama and me. I've honored it. Chris doesn't gripe and neither would she. So just look into it, counselor."

Dan didn't like confrontations, and he always liked to end on a grace note. He smiled, as if he were saving me from more grief.

"Now, is there anything else I can do for you?"

I shifted my focus, thought about it.

"Maybe."

As the notebook demonstrated, Irish Dan knew people, and he was always willing to help me in the same way he'd helped out Jade—for a price.

"Yeah, it's just a hunch."

Dan looked at me and waited.

"His name is Phillip Knott. Lives in Richmond, or near it."

"What do you need?"

"Everything."

Dan folded his hands on the table.

"Got anything else?"

"He works for the state corporation commission. Bureau of Insurance. I met him for lunch at the Shirlington Grand last week."

"Shirlington, huh? You tryin' your hand at domestic relations?"

"Could be."

Irish Dan stared at me and waited.

"The son of a bitch tried to bribe me, Dan. You know I won't stand for that."

"I remember. When do you need it?"

"Soon as you can."

It was Tuesday.

"Why don't you come back Thursday around two?"

"Jade working then?"

"I'll see that she is."

I shook his hand and decided not to wait for her next set.

***

I had a few corporate clients, local businesses I had set up and sometimes helped with the required annual compliance issues that most small businesses ignore, such as annual meetings of shareholders, the election of officers and directors, stock transfers and the like. The corporate stock book for several of these businesses resided in a bookcase in my office. And there, bound in a maroon-papered cardboard box, I found the three-ring binder I was looking for: "Barkley and Crowley, Inc. dba Riding Time."

I pulled the binder out and laid it open on my desk. In the stock register in the back, I found copies of the share certificates, showing that Christine Barkley and Dante Crowley each owned fifty shares. Though the Virginia statute required corporations to hold meetings every year to elect officers and directors, Riding Time hadn't held a meeting in seven years; at least not one that was reflected in the book.

At that meeting years ago, Dan had been elected treasurer and Ms. Barkley president. As soon as I shut the book and put it back on the shelf, I sunk into thought, but before I could get anywhere I heard a tapping at the door. It was DP Tran, his nicotine-stained teeth turned up in a smile.

"Mitch paid the rent."

"His bets must have paid off."

"I owe you one, cowboy."

"I'll keep it in mind."

Chapter Five

The Lady's View

To curious inquirers, I normally described Heather Burke, the county's chief prosecutor, as an old friend and left it at that, but she was much more. I convinced myself from time to time that I was over her, but in quiet moments she still bounded back into my thoughts. It usually didn't take much of a problem to lead me to her corner office at the top of the Arlington courthouse.

On this occasion, Betty, her secretary, was busy at the copy machine. I nodded to her and let myself in to the inner sanctum.

Heather tilted her pretty head and sneered as she pointed to a stiff armchair.

"You know you're the only person in the bar with the nerve to stroll in here unannounced?"

I sat down and crossed my legs. Subtle red tints rendered her blonde hair an intoxicating strawberry color, just as they had on the day I first met her, and though I suspected it no longer glowed without the aid of a beauty shop, I was still mesmerized.

"I try not to abuse that privilege."

That seemed to satisfy her.

"The only time you come see me anymore is when something's eating at you."

Heather and I had come up together as young lawyers. Before long, we were trying cases against each other by day and sleeping together at night. Then, she made the smart move and left me for a stable, responsible guy with a good business. I sometimes wondered if he became stable and responsible because he married her.

She still looked as cute as I remembered her as a green prosecutor handling misdemeanors. But those days were long ago, as much a part of the past as the B-52s or The Talking Heads.

"Actually, I came to see you about a case."

I thought she looked disappointed, but I was probably flattering myself.

"What kind of case?"

"Misdemeanor A&B."

Her brow furrowed.

"Every assault and battery is assigned to an assistant. I'm sure one of them has this one."

"That's true."

"But you'd rather deal with me."

She almost smiled.

"That's no secret."

She dropped her gaze and looked out the window. Her office offered a slightly better view than mine; her east-facing windows looked down on the Lincoln Memorial and the Capitol across the river. I had a sterling view of a Dunkin' Donuts.

"The case is *Commonwealth v. Tedesco*."

"Oh yes. One of Dan Crowley's girls."

"You could have charged it as malicious wounding. In fact, you could have charged it as a felony."

This was our customary dance, and I watched Heather's face as she tried to anticipate where I was taking her.

"Possibly."

"I was wondering why you didn't."

"I'm sure you've got a theory, Joth."

"I do. Chris Barkley wanted it that way. He wants a quick plea so he can move on with his life. And if Miss Tedesco pleads guilty to a misdemeanor, that's an admission of liability, so he can use it against her in the civil case that's sure to follow."

"Can't blame him for that."

"Come on, Heather. A criminal charge shouldn't be used for leverage in a civil case."

She always took offense at any suggestion that her prosecutorial motives were less than pure.

"Take it to the assistant, Joth. It's her case; it's her call."

"You know we'll have to try it."

"You going to trot out that 'he propositioned me' defense? Christ, Joth, she's practically a call girl."

Now she was baiting me, and I fought the urge to react.

"She's entitled to the same protections as anybody else."

"Make your point," she said, her patience draining away.

"I'm sure you don't know this, but a year ago, Chris's wife was granted a divorce in Henrico County on the basis of physical cruelty. I've seen the Complaint. I can get you a copy if you need it."

"So?"

"That's exculpatory evidence."

"Exculpatory evidence tends to prove innocence."

"And that's what this is, Heather. His history of physical violence toward women tends to prove her innocence in this case. That makes it admissible."

"Okay, you've got the information. What of it?"

"Does he really want to go to trial and get cross-examined on that? I assume he moved back here to get a new start."

She took a deep breath and expelled it slowly.

"What happened to you, Joth? You were the rare defense lawyer who cared about justice. What happened to that guy?"

"He's still here, still fixing your mistakes."

She moved the paperweights on her desk.

"She willing to plead to a lesser offense?"

"She's not going to plead guilty to anything. And I want him to agree to a twelve-month protective order. No contact between him and Miss Tedesco. No exceptions."

She made a dismissive sound and waived her hand.

"Get ready for trial."

"You talk to your guy or have your assistant do it. You know where to find me."

I got up.

"Nice doing business with you."

I took one more glance at Heather's hair and left.

***

Back in my office, I decided to put Jade's case aside and turn my attention back to Track. The logical next step was to contact Mrs. Moriarty, the elderly widow Track had sold part of the policy to, but before I could organize an approach, she called me. Or rather, her son-in-law did.

Three days a week, Mitch and I shared the services of Marie, a sharp-eyed, discrete retiree who answered the phone and gave us each two hours of clerical and administrative assistance. Marie took the call and announced him as Gray Grayson.

"I've been told you represent Mr. Racker?" he began without introduction.

The voice sounded animated and excited. I ventured a safe guess.

"You spoke to Mr. Knott?"

"Yeah, he called my mom."

I wanted to slow him down.

"Your mom is Mrs. Moriarty?"

"Knott just wants to make sure no one gets hurt."

"So do I."

"Your guy, Racker? He's a predator."

"Who put that idea in your head?"

The flippant tone set him off.

"Well, isn't he?"

"I've known Halftrack Racker for years, and I've never heard that word associated with him, except on a lacrosse field."

"A predator's a predator."

"I don't think you're being completely fair."

"What does a 75-year-old woman need with a policy on someone else's life?"

I made a mental note of her age.

"Mrs. Moriarty is your mom?"

"I call her my mom. She's my wife's mom, and that's the same in our family. I want everyone to know that she's unhappy. Everyone. She's known Mr. Racker since he was a child."

"Family friend?"

"Neighbors. Can you imagine that? She babysat him as a kid."

"I'm sure the relationship is important to Mr. Racker, too."

"I'll bet."

"Let's talk about what she wants."

"It's simple, really."

I could hear him take a breath before dropping his indignant tone.

"Mom wouldn't have gone to the state at all if she could have gotten Mr. Racker to just pay attention. She's paid him more than $1,000, and she hasn't even got a signed contract."

"I'm sure it's an oversight."

"That's what he said. She thought that for a long time, too, but I don't. Now, she just wants her money back. Plus, interest and costs, of course."

I wondered who'd been advising him.

"It's a pretty valuable policy."

"She's making monthly payments on it as it is. Or she's supposed to. What good is that? She's older than the guy who's insured!"

"How many siblings does your wife have?"

"None. She's an only child."

"The policy is for her benefit, after all, and yours."

He paused.

"How's it helping me?"

"Where do you think that $50,000 is going? What else could your mom be intending to do with it? Here's the thing that Mr. Racker's been wrestling with. As it stands now, if Carter dies, your mom gets her share of the proceeds from the policy and they'd probably pass to your wife in your mom's will. You know what that means—probate costs, taxes, you know the drill. Have you thought about that?"

"Well . . ."

"I'm sure he explained it to Alice. What we need to do is make your wife the beneficiary of your mother-in-law's share of the policy. Then, the proceeds go directly to her, and you. No probate, no mess."

"I don't know."

"Your mom's share was a tenth, right? That's $50,000 tax free to you. Carter's over 60, and he smokes. He's not going to live forever."

"I suppose not."

"All she needs to do is make the monthly premium payments, like she promised to . . ."

"Those payments are hard on her. She's on a fixed income."

I thought fast.

"Would she take a little bit less, maybe eight percent, if there were no further payments?"

"She'll get eight percent of the policy when Carter dies?"

"Exactly. Can we work it out along those terms?"

"How much is that?"

"Eight percent of half a million is forty thousand dollars."

I heard his breath escape, but he covered it quickly.

"I'll have to talk to mom."

"Of course."

***

On Thursday, I showed up at Riding Time, as promised. I was lucky. I just missed Jade's set. She dropped into the booth I occupied as I waited for Irish Dan.

"Looks like you could use a drink," I said.

"You want to get me fired?"

"I meant a Coke."

A moment later, the waitress put one down and re-filled my coffee cup without being asked.

"How long you think a girl can do this job?"

I looked across the room to the girl on the main stage. She was fit, but even in the flattering lighting, tell-tale sags were evident in the backs of her arms and shoulders. I also knew Dan had a hard time finding girls as slim and attractive as Jade.

"How long do you want to keep going?"

"I've got other plans. I started out just trying to pay the rent, but the money's pretty good, you know?"

"That's how it is with most jobs."

"Including yours?"

"That's what I like about you, Jade. You've got a way of getting to the heart of things."

It was only one of the things I liked about her.

When Dan arrived, he shooed her away impatiently. He didn't object to my little flirtation; he just didn't want other patrons to assume that sort of stuff went on in his establishment.

"Interesting guy, this Phillip Knott," Dan said.

"Yeah?"

I took a sealed envelope out of my jacket pocket and pushed it across to him. He took it and pocketed it without opening it.

"He leases a Porsche and makes hefty payments on it. Living high on the hog on middle manager money."

He raised an eyebrow significantly.

"Lives off Parham Road."

That didn't sound like a middle-class address.

"Married?"

"Ten years, two kids. Wife doesn't work. Kids go to private school."

"Does his wife come from money?"

"You want a lot for $300, Joth."

"Yes, I do."

He scowled, and I laughed.

"You'd do this for free, Dan, and you know it."

He chuckled and shrugged.

"Beats running a bar. You want the kicker?"

"He's got a girlfriend up here?"

"Better. He's got a boyfriend."

I whistled.

"We talkin' about the same guy?"

"Works for the SCC, right?"

"Dan, don't ever let anyone tell you you're not worth the money."

He dropped the notebook in front of me, then laughed and wandered off to make sure no one was gambling in the pool room. Jade gave him a chance to clear out and reclaimed her seat.

I grinned and dialed up a question.

"Jade, what kind of car do you suppose I drive?"

"Something conservative. BMW."

"Is that what you expect a lawyer to drive?"

"Sure."

"What kind of guy drives a Porsche?"

"My kind of guy."

"You wouldn't like this guy."

"Why not?"

"He likes boys."

"Who?"

"Just some guy I asked Dan about."

"I got no patience for that," she said.

She sounded more grave than what I expected of a stripper in a negligee.

"Bad for business?"

She sneered contemptuously.

"What's the perv's name?"

"You wouldn't know him. He lives in Richmond."

"Those people disgust me."

I took a look around her little sanctuary.

"When did you find religion?"

The word religion seemed to set her off. "You think I can't have standards because I take my clothes off for men?

"Can't say I ever thought about it."

The conversation had gone further than I wanted it to. Since I was unable to dredge up another topic, I apologized and got up to go.

***

It rained on Monday and looked like it would keep up for a week. At nine o'clock, as I scurried across Clarendon Boulevard, a north wind drove the downpour in sheets. General District Court was on the third floor of the courthouse, and Jade was waiting for me on a wooden bench outside the courtroom. We exchanged hellos as I shook out my raincoat.

"Is he here?"

The staging area outside the courtroom wasn't much bigger than a handball court, and it was crowded with defendants and those who would determine their fate. All I could see were long faces, impatient witnesses, and defense attorneys scurrying around trying to put their cases together on the fly.

Jade nodded toward the far end of the room.

"In the blue blazer."

Chris Barkley was standing in a corner, hands jammed in his pockets, his shoulders hunched, as he listened to Sue Cranwell, a young assistant DA with a stack of files in her hands. He nodded, and she jotted something on the top file and turned a page.

I tried to recall Mama Barkley's face.

"Come on, Jade, let's go inside and sit."

The large, high-ceilinged courtroom featured dark wood paneling and furnishings and modern technology, the kind of place that intimidates dishonest witnesses and reluctant parties. Jade was understandably anxious. We'd met on Friday to review her possible testimony and she'd done well. She was used to being on the stage after all, and she wasn't shy.

"Don't worry," I said. "You're ready to go."

"Absolutely."

Several of her co-workers were on call if needed.

"Any questions?"

She shook her head.

"There is one thing," she said. "I know Dan's paying. I feel kind of bad about that. Can I make you dinner?"

"I'm not sure that's a good idea, Jade. Let's see how today goes."

"Oh, are you one of those guys who's too good for strippers?"

"I'm not too good for anybody."

***

Sitting so close to Jade, the minutes felt like hours, but it wasn't long before I felt the tap on my shoulder. Cranwell was about the same age Heather was when she tried her first case. A pretty woman, but unlike Heather, she was a full-bodied brunette who was anxious in the courtroom.

"Got a minute?"

Her breath was sour from too much coffee.

"Sure."

We found a quiet place in the corner of the hallway.

"You're right, he doesn't want to go to trial. But he will."

"Why?"

"Because she needs to be sanctioned for what she did."

"He beat up his wife and didn't get sanctioned for that. He ought to consider the ledger square."

She raised her chin toward the file under my arm.

"That evidence is not going to come in."

"The hell it's not."

I was relishing the challenge from this upstart rookie. Heather would've appreciated her moxie. In fact, I wouldn't have been surprised if Heather had prepped her for our encounter.

I opened up my folder and showed Cranwelll a certified copy of Barkley's former wife's divorce Compliant and the Final Decree.

"It's public record and it's relevant. It's getting in. You can spend the rest of the morning explaining it to the judge, 'cause there's no good answer to it. I want a dismissal."

"Let me talk to him," she said, turning away.

I went back inside. It was 9:30 when she got back to me.

"All right, we'll drop it."

"And the protective order?"

"Not a chance."

"All rise."

The door behind the raised bench opened, and the judge strode in.

"This honorable court for the County of Arlington, Virginia is now in session. All those having business before the court draw near. The honorable Richard Hawkins, presiding."

Hawkins was a brisk, efficient man. The first cases he called would be the agreed dismissals, but even those required Cranwell's attention. She approached me as we all stood up.

"Six months on the protective order," she whispered.

"Done."

As she opened the gate and walked into the well of the court, she addressed the bench.

"Your honor, would you call *Commonwealth v. Tedesco*? I think that's an agreed dismissal."

Ten minutes later, I was back out in the rain.

"That's it?" Jade said. "It's all over?"

"Yes. And if you see him again, you let me know. He's not going to bother you anymore."

She glowed with gratitude and vigorous good health, as if she'd just received a new lease on her young life.

"We'll have to do that dinner, Joth."

"Maybe."

"I owe you, you know. I don't forget."

"I appreciate it. I'll see you around the place."

***

Track was waiting in the reception area when I got back, turning the pages of a hunting magazine Mitch subscribed to. For a moment, I imagined his face among the black and white portraits of Lee's Lieutenants. With that fierce expression in his dark eyes, you could put him in gray wool with a wreathed star on each side of a stand-up collar and he would have fit right in. He held up the magazine and pointed proudly to a photo of a six-point buck.

"I got one like that in the valley last winter."

"Is that where you got the hide for those cowboy boots?"

He glared, and I remembered something I'd been told about Track, that he had no tolerance for banter unless he was serving it up.

"Why don't you get yourself a decent suit?"

"Gray flannel not good enough for you?"

He regarded me with the expression of scorn which I remembered from our first meeting.

"Christ, Joth, that cut of suit hasn't been in style for ten years."

He was probably right, but his sour response and penchant for personal animus were of no concern to me. They were just some of the things that made him a bad teammate. I looked at the clock over the credenza.

"You're early."

He took a gulp of air.

"Didn't mean to be."

"Not a problem. Come on in."

As he sat down, he tossed an unsealed envelope on my desk. Inside was the agreement between Track and Alice Moriarty, the exact one I'd been nagging him about. I immediately noticed a couple of things wrong with it.

"This isn't signed."

"I signed it."

"Don't make me laugh, Track."

He scowled.

"You know who Gray Grayson is?"

"Yeah, he's trouble."

"He says he's just trying to help."

"Same as me," Track said.

"Grayson's the guy who blew the whistle and got Knott involved."

"The son of a bitch," said Track. "He shouldn't have done that."

I held up the contract.

"This might have something to do with it."

"I don't get it."

"I'm sure you don't."

I studied the contract again. It was a two-page document, reasonably written, proper and in order, requiring Mrs. Moriarty, to make monthly payments to Track until Carter's death, when the policy would pay off.

"Track, she's paying you $100 a month? What are the premiums?"

"About twice that."

I looked at him over the top of the contract.

89

"She's paying half the premiums, but she only gets 10 percent of the proceeds?"

"It's still a good deal."

"For who?" I said.

It was a shabby deal at best. I shook my head and let it go. Track had signed and dated the contract.

"How come she didn't sign it?"

"She did."

"Okay, let's have it."

"She's got it."

"You didn't keep a copy?"

"We signed it on her kitchen table. It's not like she has a copy machine."

"Yeah? She says she didn't sign it."

"Well, she's lying. Or Grayson is. You talk to Alice?"

"No," I said, realizing I probably should have.

"He's lying," Track said. "That's what he does."

I shrugged, looking for more, but Track clammed up.

"Of course, if Mrs. Moriarty didn't have it, it would explain why she wanted out."

"If she wanted out, it would explain why she suddenly can't find it."

"That's your story and you're sticking to it."

"That's right, Joth. And now I've got the state on my back."

"If you won't give her the money back, what else is she going to do? Unless she picks a bone with you, her choice is to keep paying you and trust in your generosity and risk that you might stiff her."

His eyes widened. The idea amazed him.

"She knows I'm not going to stiff her. I've known her all my life."

I scowled at him.

"You can put this behind you today if you really want to."

"Yeah?"

"Two ways. Give her back the money she paid you."

"I told you, I haven't got it."

"Or give her a formal assignment of her portion of the policy."

"She doesn't want that."

"I think she'll take it."

"What if she stops paying me?"

"I can take care of that."

Track leaned in to listen, something he rarely did.

"What if you give her a reduced amount, say $45,000, in return for forgiving the rest of the payments?"

"Phil Knott doesn't want that either."

"The guy who doesn't want to do it is you. You don't want to cut her in on the big payday when Carter dies."

"You're telling me that Knott will go along with this?"

"That's my job."

"You said he's Old Virginia. What do you know about this guy?"

"Knott? I know he lives way beyond his means. Drives a Porsche and sends his kids to private schools."

Track paused. His head tilted as he absorbed this information.

"How do you know that?"

"Because I pay attention."

"Let me think about it?"

"What's there to think about?"

"The future."

***

He called me from his car less than 10 minutes later.

"Okay, Joth but eight percent. That's $40,000. That's plenty for what she paid."

"You mean, give her a contract? No more payments?"

"If that's what it takes, yeah. I can't afford to take her out."

"Poor choice of words."

"I guess," he said. "You get assurances from Knott first. Make sure if I do this, my problem goes away."

I agreed. I was more concerned about that than Track. For some reason, I felt as if I might have more to lose if this deal went south.

Chapter Six

Del Ray

It wasn't that I didn't want to go out with Jade; I just didn't think it was prudent. Dan Crowley was my biggest and steadiest source of business, and I couldn't afford to mess it up. Of course, I reasoned, it would be just as easy to mess it up if I appeared to be insulting one of his girls.

As I knew from the warrant, Jade was twelve years younger than me, but this was another excuse I opted to decline. She had offered to make me dinner and that allowed me the flexibility to pack it in if I saw things getting dangerous. She was pretty, and I liked her, so I agreed.

Jade shared half a duplex in Del Ray with a girl named Gala Thompson. I had trouble finding it, and even more trouble parking, which made me late. That meant my carefully constructed suave façade had slipped by the time I rang her bell.

She came to the door dressed demurely in a skirt and sweater. I apologized for being late and commented on the broad porch she and her roommate apparently shared with their neighbor.

"It used to be a single-family home when all this was farmland," she said, with an expansive wave at the encroaching bungalows.

She took the bouquet of early spring flowers I'd picked up on the drive over and sniffed them approvingly.

I was still looking at her sweater.

"He divided it up into four apartments, and I don't think anybody's complaining."

"Who's 'he?' "

"Dan. I thought you knew that."

"Dan Crowley?"

Jade bit her lower lip.

"He owns a lot of places around here."

"Can't say it surprises me," I said disguising my surprise.

Jade's unit inside the old farmhouse occupied one side of the first floor. It was narrow but deep, with two bedrooms and a bath in the back and a kitchenette separated by an arched walkway from a dinette. Its living room opened onto the porch.

I watched Jade carry the bouquet back to the kitchen to put in a vase and soon smelled the delicious scents of simmering tomato sauce and Italian spices. She'd gone to some trouble with her hair, highlighting the natural copper tone to an enticing degree and styling it with a flip. Combined with her clothes, it proclaimed a girlish innocence, and for the first time I realized she was self-conscious about her line of work.

"Roommate around?"

"Gala? Nope. Out with her boyfriend. Always out with her boyfriend. Must be nice."

"She works for Dan?"

"Yeah, but not at the place. She's a bartender at Dan's sport pub over on 23rd Street."

Jade peeked at my expression as she primped the flowers.

"You didn't know Dan owned the pub, did you?"

"Dan's got his hand in a lot of things."

"Well, I guess he does."

She carried the vase into the dinette and placed it in the center of small table set for two.

"Drink?"

"Of course. What are you having?"

"Margarita?"

I'd noticed the blender on the counter and knew I couldn't say no.

"I hope you like Italian?"

"Love it."

"I'm making stuffed shells and sausages."

She gestured toward the sideboard in the dinette.

"Why don't you get a chair and talk to me while I'm cooking?"

I watched her walk back to the kitchen. Dan teaches them how to walk when they first come on board. He does an excellent job.

As I grabbed one of the two ladder-back chairs from the dinette table, I noticed a business card tucked under a basket of red apples on the crowded sideboard. It read *Frank P. Racker, Registered Investment Advisor*. I turned it over: nothing on the back. I left it there, carried the chair into the kitchen and placed it where I could sit and study Jade's profile.

As the shells baked in the oven, she prepared a green salad and transferred each item to a wooden bowl.

"Tedesco. Southern Italy?"

"As Italian as the pope. That's what my mom used to say when we were little. 'Course that doesn't work anymore."

Not only did Jade alter her appearance away from the place; her pattern of speech was different as well. Gone were the punkish phrases and mannerisms, as if she could swap vernacular as easily as clothing. I hadn't known her last name or her given first name until I'd seen them on the warrant.

"Do your friends call you Jade or Jennifer?"

She shot me a surprised look, but figured it out quickly and smiled that dimpled smile.

"My real friends don't know me from the place. They call me Jenny. Except my brother."

"What does he call you?"

She sighed.

"There's a lot of disappointment there. He's a priest."

"A priest?"

My reaction annoyed her.

"Catholic priest. He's assistant rector at St. Carolyn's in Arlington. People think I drove him to it, but if anything, it's the other way around. Anyway, call me Jenny. I'd much prefer that."

"Might take a while to get used to it."

"You can call me Jade around the place."

"I don't even know where you're from, Jenny."

"Eastern Shore of Maryland. Conservative Catholic family. They'll be glad when I give up working at the place."

"Is that something you're thinking about?"

She considered her answer and it occurred to me that she feared any confidence might be revealed to Dan.

"This is an attorney-client privileged communication," I said.

"Yes," she said, after releasing a laugh.

"What are you going to do?"

"Finish school," she said.

Her response was bold and clear, and she sounded happy to disclose it.

"I've always wanted to be a nurse. They say it's hard on your feet, but it can't be worse than what I do now."

"Nursing school?"

She caught a note of disbelief in my voice and seemed to resent it. I wanted her to hear encouragement in my voice.

"Why this year?"

"I just needed to put the money together."

Her frown softened, as if she was used to skeptics.

"I'm getting close. I've got my applications in. Then I won't have to do this anymore."

"When will you hear?"

Jenny looked at the calendar on the back of the kitchen door and jabbed her finger at a circled date.

"It's all electronic these days. When the time comes, you just log in and there it is. I'm a little nervous, to tell you the truth."

She shot me a quick glance.

"A lot of the girls at the place, they're all in. It's their career. You know, I'm the only girl there who doesn't have any tattoos? Any."

She examined my expression.

99

"You know what a tramp stamp is?"

I shrugged a little.

"Everyone has one there, but not me."

She turned away from me, bent forward and flipped up the tail of her sweater and shirt, revealing a crescent of smooth, taut and unmarked flesh.

"When I put this behind me, it'll be behind me."

It was just growing dark when she took the shells and sausages out of the oven and by then we'd each finished two margaritas. I found a box of wooden matches and lit two candles on the dinette table.

"It's been a long time since I've had a meal as nice as this."

As I pulled out her chair, I smelled her perfume.

"Or with a girl as nice as you."

"You're sweet," she said. "I always knew you were sweet."

I knew stuffed shells as a back-of-the-box recipe, but it's all in the sauce, and Jenny's was beyond my experience: sweet and artfully spiced, with a wine that matched it, at least as far as I could tell. We talked more about nursing school and growing up on the Eastern Shore, but my curiosity got the better of me.

"Do you know Track Racker?"

"I don't know who you mean."

I reached behind me for the business card.

She took it from me and nodded at it.

"Oh him. Sure, he comes around. We all know him as Frank. A night owl, not like you."

"How do you happen to have his card?"

"He gives it out."

She shook her head.

"People are always giving us cards."

"Did he sell you a policy?"

"A policy?"

"An annuity or an insurance policy?"

Jenny wrinkled her nose.

"I couldn't afford what he sells. Gala bought one though."

"Bought what?"

"I don't know. Some sort of life insurance policy. He's got the golden tongue, that guy. Or something like that."

"Like him?"

She shifted her posture and pushed her hands up through her hair.

"I didn't know he was a friend of yours."

"He's not. What do you think of him?"

"He's all right. He's always flashing a lot of money and talking about his southern heritage. Course we're all willing to listen if the tips are good. He's a little scary to tell the truth, but his money's green and it folds."

"Scary, how?"

"You're making me nervous, Joth, asking all of these questions."

"Sorry. That's what I do."

"Can't you leave work behind tonight?"

She smiled, but I could read the annoyance in her eyes.

I let my breath ease out.

"You're right, you know. A lot of guys with bigger practices than me have no problem leaving it at their desk."

"He's a client?"

I put my fork down.

"You see, what I do isn't brain surgery. Most of my cases follow a pattern, and I can do them in my sleep. But every once in a while, I get one where something's just not right. Those are the ones I can't put down."

"That's Frank's case?"

I squirmed for a second and fished for a neutral answer.

"I want it to come out right, Jenny. It's important to me."

"If you do as well as you did for me . . ."

"That case was important to me, too. But for a different reason."

She held my eyes, and I knew in that moment I had crossed a frontier. I didn't know if it was wise, but I didn't regret it.

After dinner, I helped her clear the dishes.

"Dessert?"

She asked in a way that seemed mischievous.

"What are you offering?"

I leaned forward to kiss her and she responded like she'd been as hungry for that moment as I was. She took my hand, but instead of taking me back to her bedroom, led me into the living room and onto the couch beneath the broad bay window. There were people out in the street and plenty of noise, but the lights lent a relaxing low glow to the room. I kissed her again.

"I thought you'd never get around to this," she said.

"I've always been slow to figure out what's good for me."

Once committed, I was committed all the way, but she was prudent and careful, and soon she pushed me away.

"I think that's enough for tonight, don't you?"

"No."

My lack of restraint empowered her.

"Well, it is. A girl like me has to be careful or she'll get a reputation."

I reached for her again.

"I'm not going to give you a reputation."

She laughed and stood up.

"I know. But not tonight."

Jenny looked at me and responded to something in my expression.

"Soon."

Chapter Seven

Toiling in the Vineyard

The time had come to pay a call on Alice Moriarty. I had her address in the file, but the following day I called and asked Track for it anyway. I wanted to gauge his reaction to the inquiry, and he didn't disappoint.

"You don't want to go see her, Joth."

"Why not?"

"She's old and feeble."

"But competent enough for you to sell her a viatical she didn't need?"

"Listen, that was a long time ago. Back then, she wanted it and she knew why."

"Really? Why?"

Track didn't respond.

"I told both Grayson and Knott it was for estate planning purposes. You know, to secure the next generation. I hope I was telling the truth."

"That's exactly right."

"That's what I thought you'd say."

***

Alice Moriarty was asleep when I got there. I figured the guy who met me at the door was Grayson, a slender 30-year-old with washed out features and a blond porn-star mustache.

"You should have called," he said.

He had the pugnacious tone of a rancher defending his spread.

I raised my hands apologetically.

"Didn't have the number. Can I come in?"

He kept his hand on the door. He didn't step back, but he didn't shut it either.

"I need to know she's protected."

"That's the only reason for me to be here. You know that."

Grayson peeked over his shoulder at the narrow stairs to the second floor.

"She ought to be down soon," he said, and held open the door.

We sat at a circular faux-wood table wedged into the corner of a small kitchen. He offered me coffee and I accepted a cup that tasted like it had been in the glass carafe about a week.

"Day off today?"

"I'm between jobs at the moment."

I nodded sympathetically.

"From talking to Track – Mr. Racker – it seems like you've got your hands full caring for Alice."

He thought about it before agreeing.

"She's aged quickly the last few years."

"You know, if she wants out of that viatical . . ."

"No. What you said makes sense. She's got enough. She wants to make sure her daughter is provided for."

"She around?"

"She's at work. Be home around four."

I heard scuffling sounds from upstairs, and Grayson's ears perked up like a bloodhound.

"That'll be Alice."

He excused himself and hurried up the hall stairs, giving me an opportunity to look around. It was a tiny split-level; the kind they stopped building in the sixties, and I guessed that's when Alice and her late husband bought it. The paint on the walls was scuffed and faded, and much of the furniture showed markings of similar abuse. The rest of it belonged to a cheap teak set that looked like it had been shoehorned in when the person who owned it was forced to relocate. Every flat surface in the kitchen and adjacent living room was crowded with framed photographs. Most featured the same woman, aging progressively while the young girl with her grew and the man aged until he disappeared from the more recent photos, to be replaced by Gray Grayson.

They had a boxy color TV and lottery tickets stuck out from between the pages of catalogues.

When I heard them on the stairs, I resumed my seat in the kitchen, rising as Alice entered on Grayson's arm.

"Good afternoon, Mrs. Moriarty."

She nodded.

It seemed to take all of her concentration to get herself situated on the chair. Beside it was a pack of Marlboros. Her son-in-law shook one out and lit it for her with a Bic lighter.

"I appreciate you taking the time."

"Got nothing else to do," she said, through a long drag.

"This man is Frank's lawyer," Grayson said, pointing at me.

"About Frank," I began, but she waved the cigarette at me.

"Oh, he's all right. Just the same as the rest of us. Gray here, he just tries to take care of me."

"I guess the question is, what do you want to do about this policy that Mr. Racker got for you?"

"Do you think I look like someone who needs a life insurance policy?"

"Why did you buy it?"

"Frank said it would be a good idea. He's always advised me wise."

"He says maybe we misunderstood the man," Grayson said.

He reached forward and patted Alice on her hand. She huffed at her son-in-law, pulling her arm away.

"*You* misunderstood him you mean."

"He says maybe he was doing estate planning."

She took another deep drag.

"I don't have an estate."

"Mrs. Moriarty," I said, "I don't mean to interrupt, but what I mean is, Frank may have intended the policy to provide for your family. Your heirs."

"After I die, you mean."

"Frank's too delicate a guy to put it that way."

"You're right."

She coughed.

"He never mentioned it."

I snuck a peek at Grayson, who looked like a truant schoolboy.

"Frank will do what you want: cancel it, cash it out, give you a contract. The only reason you'd want to keep it is to take care of your family after you're gone."

"Do what you think best, Mom. We'll get by."

Alice looked at her son-in-law and blinked, scanned the room, and then looked at me. I held her gaze. It was easy after that.

***

I did not have the type of legal practice that generated long-term professional relationships. My typical clients were discomfited, disillusioned and disaffected people looking for someone to blame for the price exacted by their personal failings. Most viewed a lawyer as a further intrusion of a rigged system. More often than not, they were aware of their guilt, even if they refused to acknowledge it, and they cooperated with me with the wary ambivalence that one customarily extends to a midway gamesman looking for shills at a local carnival.

The only drop-ins I ever got were sad-sack defendants reduced to asking court personnel to recommend a good, cheap, defense lawyer. When I heard the door open, I assumed that someone of that description had walked into the reception area.

Just two days after that perfect Italian dinner, my mood lifted when I stepped out of my office and saw Jenny.

"Secretary out today?"

"She's part-time. Today's her day off."

Behind her, a dark-haired man stood gazing out the window with his hands clasped behind his back. At the sound of my voice, he turned. He was wearing dark slacks and a dark, short-sleeve shirt with a Roman collar. Jenny extended her hand toward him.

"Joth, this is my brother, Father John."

He wasn't the first priest who'd ever set foot in my office. I stepped forward and shook the outstretched hand.

"Just John, please," he said, with a pleasant laugh that dimpled his face.

I saw the resemblance in the shape of the face and the Mediterranean complexion. "John, it is."

"My sister said you took care of her."

"Not yet."

I took a certain pride in my ability to engage in meaningless banter without awkwardness or mistake, but it was only after these words had spilled out that I realized what I'd said, and I was unable to find a decent means of recalling them.

"Don't be troubled, Joth. That's what we get for dropping by unannounced."

"Well, I didn't mean . . ."

I turned to Jenny. She was dressed in a plain green sweatshirt and a pair of jeans with dirty knees.

"What brings the two of you over here?"

Jenny looked at her feet. My careless comment had embarrassed her more than it had her brother.

"In the area," she said. "Literally."

John looked at his sister and grinned.

"I assure you I'm not checking up on my sister's friends. I'm the assistant rector over at St. Carolyn's."

He jerked his thumb over his shoulder in a westerly direction.

"Jenny's not been as attentive as I'd like about Mass, but she's makes up for it by toiling in the vineyards of the Lord."

She rolled her eyes.

"I help with the gardening."

"She's got quite a green thumb," John said.

"It's her best color."

To my relief, John laughed gamely, and Jenny smiled.

"We were just walking by," she said, "on the way to Whole Foods."

I looked at my watch. It was too early for lunch.

"Come in and have a seat. Something to drink?"

They looked at each other and shook their heads as I escorted them into my office.

I assumed John was aware of the age difference between his sister and me and was here to count the tree rings inside my tired and gnarled bark. He gave the impression of a man of instinctive caution, but also of a man comfortable with himself. He waited for his sister

to sit, then followed suit while casting a quick, evalua-
tive look around my stark and spartan office.

"This is a comfortable place."

"You think so?"

"I do. Unpretentious. Simple. Clean."

He leaned forward and folded his hands between his
knees.

"A place to inspire confidence. Our businesses are
perhaps alike in some ways."

The lack of frills reflected the state of my bank account and not an effort to assuage the concerns of the
afflicted.

"Oh? How's that?"

He reacted to my tone by straightening up.

"Nothing profound, I assure you. People come to me, bur-
dened by . . ."

He turned up his hands and wagged his head, set-
tling for the obvious word.

"Guilt. Yes. Mistakes they've made, bad choices.
You and I, we both help people recover from the cost of
those bad choices, don't you think?"

I squirmed in my chair, not sure where he was
headed.

"I provide a very limited comfort, compared to
you."

"Nonsense."

A mask of seriousness suddenly descended over his features.

"For one thing, everyone believes in the comfort you provide. My clients, if you will, are gambling on a pay-off in the next life."

He nodded heavily, as if assessing the odds.

"That's a long bet, don't you think?"

The frankness of his admission startled me.

"I'm not sure I've heard a priest put it that way before."

"Let me get to the point. It's not unusual for me to hear things, like concerns and disturbing stories. It's a sad litany. I need someone to refer those people to, and Jenny raves about your work."

"You mean people facing criminal charges?"

"Potentially, yes. I could send them to you, if they felt they needed legal help."

"I see. We can be mutual referral sources. Is that what you're suggesting?"

"You laugh, but I know how hard it is to proselyte, especially if you don't believe it, so I'm not asking that. I just want someone I feel I can trust, when and if I have a parishioner in need. That'll help everybody, don't you think?"

"You're not going to try to drag me back to church?"

For a moment, John seemed amused by my display of skepticism, but he quickly straightened his posture and his face before responding.

"That's not part of the deal, Joth. I like to think of this as doing well by doing good, as Ben Franklin put it. Of course, if you find yourself drawn back into the fold, we'd welcome you, but there will be no pressure from me."

I'd been disappointed by people in his line of work before, but if you aren't willing to trust the next person, you become cynical, and that is the unforgivable sin. I made a show of considering the offer, and then delivered the clincher.

"I think I can help you out."

He touched an index finger to his lips thoughtfully and looked at his sister.

"See how easy it is? I wish saving souls could be so simple."

Father John twisted in the chair, making a more thorough inspection of my modest digs. He nodded, as if what he saw reinforced his conclusions about me. Then, he got up and winked at his sister.

"We'll be in touch. I see you're busy, Joth. We can let ourselves out."

Jenny and I nodded good-bye.

I waited until I heard the outer door swing shut, then sat at my desk, musing about this unlikely meeting. I wasn't the sort to credit everything a priest said just because he wore a collar, and something about Father John didn't sit right with me. The visit was too abrupt for him to have formed a professional opinion about me, and if he trusted his sister as much as he said he did, there was no reason to come see me in the first place. No, despite his denial, this was probably a good Italian brother looking after his sister. I didn't have a problem with that, but what I didn't like was him pretending it was something else. Then again, it could have been the reverse; that he considered his sister a lost cause and was using her to try and capitalize on some other scheme.

***

I called Phillip Knott that afternoon at the number printed on the face of his business card.

"I thought I told you to call my cell," he said, whispering as soon as he recognized my voice.

"This number seems to work."

"What's your cell?"

I gave it to him.

"I'll call you back."

It took him ten minutes to get back to me, which gave me ten minutes to think.

"You surprised me, that's all. Everything all right?"

"Sure," I said. "Just wanted to let you know that I think we can get this done along the terms you proposed."

"I think the idea was to return Ms. Moriarty's payments and cancel the transaction."

"Maybe I misheard," I said. "I thought we'd formalize her interest in the policy."

"She won't go for that."

"On the contrary."

"You've talked to her?"

"Sure have."

There was a long pause.

"I don't know, Joth. I'm all for working things out, but what if she doesn't pay him? It would only make sense for Racker to declare a default. Then, she's unhappy and my manager is unhappy, too. That's a problem I can't afford and neither can you."

"Got it covered. He's going to give her eight percent instead of 10. That means $40,000 when Carter dies. In return, Track keeps what's she's already paid and that's the end of it. No further premium payments or entanglements."

"Why would that be fair?"

"Because she's acquired a $40,000 benefit for about a thousand dollars. She's not going to like it if you take that away from her, and neither will her son-in-law."

"Ah yes, Mr. Grayson."

Knott sighed as he shifted the phone to his other ear.

"I don't know. It's complicated. Too risky. What if Racker misses a premium payment? If he defaults, the insurance company will cancel the policy."

"Are you kidding? It's worth half a million dollars. He'd miss his mortgage payment before he'd miss a premium payment. And if he keeps his license, neither will happen. It's just good business all around."

"You're asking a lot, Joth. People will question whether I did my job."

"There's no one to ask any questions because nobody gets hurt."

He paused again. He had a lot of angles to consider.

"Racker's going to have to come up with some money."

Knott's tone had changed, and the register of his voice dropped. I knew what he was after, and I wondered how he'd work around to it.

"Is he?" I said.

"He's asking me to go above and beyond, Joth. This is clearly outside the scope of my authority."

"He's not . . ."

"But I can make it happen. Don't worry. I've got the discretion to do that."

"I see. Sounds costly."

"Not really. Not if you look at the big picture. I would just want him to recognize my efforts on his behalf."

"And how might that be expressed?"

"I think it would be remiss for me to try to quantify that."

"I see. Measured in four figures?"

"Heavens, Mr. Proctor, be reasonable. It's a half-million-dollar policy and I'm going to let him keep it."

"So, this recognition, it would come after Mr. Carter goes to his reward?"

"Oh no, that wouldn't do."

I paused, but he waited me out.

"And how do we formalize this?" I said.

"Joth, I have a carefully cultivated reputation for rectitude."

"Rectitude? As in inflexible moral standards?"

"Of course," he said.

He spoke without irony or shame. But he had a fine sense of how far to push it.

"You give it some thought, Joth, okay? There's no rush. You know where to reach me."

"On the cell."

I meant it as a dig, but he'd already hung up.

I stewed for a while, reviewing Knott's choice of words, and then called Track.

"I'll be out your way Friday. Can we get together for a drink?"

"Why?"

"Developments. I learned some interesting things about our friend, Mr. Knott."

"Beyond the fact that he tried to bribe you?"

"Let's talk it over in person."

"Why not?"

I could picture Track shrugging. He gave me the name of a bar in Old Town and we agreed on a time.

***

Jenny's "soon" from our dinner date couldn't come too soon for me. Something about her had stuck in my head like an old pop song you'd never admit you really liked. After checking her schedule with Irish Dan, I called her at home.

"I hope you weren't offended by my brother," she said.

"Not at all."

"He thinks he's tactful and diplomatic, but he's really not."

"He gets to the point."

"He thinks he can help you. But this is really about helping himself."

"That's what we're all doing, isn't it?"

"Is that why you called?"

"Not about your brother. I was wondering if you have any plans for dinner tomorrow night."

She hesitated, then said yes.

"You don't seem too excited."

"I just didn't think you'd call."

She emitted a tinkle of laughter.

"What should I wear?"

A couple of responses flitted through my head, but I was sure she had heard plenty of those around the place.

"Something simple. Something green. Something like what you wore the night you cooked me dinner."

"I think I can handle that."

I gave her a time and told her I'd pick her up. She waited for me to hang up and I got stuck doing the same, like I was back in school.

"Okay," I said, failing to come up with anything witty. "I'll see you then."

Chapter Eight

Inside Information

The restaurant adjacent to the marina at Daingerfield Island operates as Indigo Landing, a name that conjured images of South Pacific seaports trading in silks and exotic spices. Instead, it featured a gently lit, open dining room, adjacent to a long, oval bar of blonde wood. Circular two- and four-top tables were spaced discretely apart on the polished wooden floor, creating intimacy. I chose it because it was elegant and close to Del Ray. It didn't hurt that it had good food, the charm of an underappreciated treasure and a fabulous view northward up the river.

We took a table beneath a window, with an unobstructed view of the illuminated Capitol dome and the Washington Monument. I had chosen a summer-weight, navy wool suit, white shirt and green tie. Conservative and boring, perhaps, but unobjectionable and likely to suit to anything Jenny might wear.

Jade, or Jenny, as I now resolved to call her, had taken my suggestion and wore a jade green cotton dress that highlighted her eyes and hugged her curves. She had opted for a more natural look, with minimal makeup, and with the candlelight playing on her high cheekbones and tawny complexion, she looked even better without it.

"Congress is working tonight," I said, as we sat down.

"How do you know?"

I pointed out that the lamp in the dome of the Capital was lit.

"They only light it when the Senate or the House is in session."

She leaned on her elbow and put her long, well-manicured fingertips to her lips.

"What do you suppose they're talking about?"

"Couldn't care less."

She laughed and looked at me closely.

"You're not the average DC lawyer, are you?"

"No such thing as an average DC lawyer."

"You're all above average?"

It was my turn to laugh and the welcome appearance of the waiter allowed me to avoid a response.

"Drink?"

"Margarita?"

"It worked last time, didn't it?" I said, before turning to the waiter. "Two on the rocks, please."

"You didn't answer my question," Jenny said.

"You know what I like about you? You're not shy about asking questions."

"But you're shy about answering them."

I acknowledged something else I liked about her. Not since Heather had there been anyone in my life to test me and keep me honest. I understood that given a chance, she would.

"All right. The average DC lawyer is ambitious, political and cutthroat."

"You're pretty cutthroat in court."

"It's just business."

"I'm used to lawyers on TV screaming at each other."

"That's not really my style."

"Always calm and steady?"

I thought about it.

"I wouldn't say that. I can have a temper on occasion."

"Like when the other lawyer lies and cheats?"

I shrugged.

"Lawyers lie and cheat. At least some of them do. It comes with the territory, so you just deal with it. But that's not what makes me mad."

I was feeling my way toward a more complete answer. She saw this and waited.

"What sets me off is injustice. I won't stand for that. When I see it, I feel compelled to fix it."

"And how do you fix it?"

I shrugged again, not for a lack of ideas. I just wasn't sure how much I wanted to share about how things work in my messy business.

"The law is not a perfect tool, Jenny, but it's the best thing we have. At least I haven't come up with anything else."

Another waiter came and we ordered.

"Anyway, I take care of my clients and then I go home."

"What do you do then?"

"As little as possible."

"That's the ambitious part?"

I showed her a dismissive expression.

"I don't go to Rotary meetings or donate my time to charitable causes, if that's what you mean. I don't go to bar association functions or mix and mingle with the people who can refer me business."

"Why not?"

"Because I usually don't like them."

"Oh God, I hope you're not a loner."

"I'm not exactly gregarious."

"I am. I'm a people person."

What she said struck me with force. Heather had been a people person. I suddenly realized that Jenny was already dragging me out of the shell I had crawled back into over the years. I needed a people person, and there she was, sitting right across from me.

"Look, Jenny, I like people. Don't get me wrong. I'm in a people business. It's just that I don't like them when they're swapping favors and pretending to be someone they're not."

The drinks came. Jenny examined the salted rim and stirred hers thoughtfully. "People wear a lot of hats in their lives, Joth. Sometimes, those hats change for good. Look around."

I followed the flowing gesture of her hand.

"You don't know who these people are, or who they'll be tomorrow. They could be judges or opposing lawyers. Some of them could become your friends someday, or your clients."

At Dan's place, Jade communicated in the terms and lingo of her trade. In a fashionable restaurant, and dressed like the patrons around her, she fit right in as a sharp and insightful woman. Still, there was another concern I couldn't shake.

"Can I ask you a personal question?"

As soon as I asked, Jenny shrank away.

"I'm on the pill," she said.

"That wasn't my question."

"Okay," she said.

I could feel her apprehension and turned my face toward the bar for a moment to assemble the right words. I did not want to screw this up.

"Do you think I might be too old for you?"

It was a difficult question, but one that I'd been anxious to ask. No man wants to face the daunting truth that advancing age has rendered a desirable woman untouchable, and the question had nagged at me since I'd seen Jenny's date of birth on the misdemeanor warrant.

"No," she said.

Her answer was prompt and belied any apparent uncertainty on her part.

"How old do you think I am?"

"I don't know. Thirty-two, thirty-three."

"I'm thirty-seven."

"So?"

"So, you'll be twenty-six in November."

"You ask too many questions."

"Maybe. But I'll be thirty-eight by then. I'm twelve years older than you, no matter how you look at it."

"So?"

"So, it may not matter now, but what about when I'm fifty and you're still 38?"

She laughed that delightful tinkling little laugh of hers.

"Oh, okay, are we getting married?"

It was my turn to blush.

"Okay, you've got me there," I said.

While her point remained valid, I didn't want to get into a relationship with an automatic expiration date, and neither should she.

"You're going to think about this differently one of these days."

Jenny smirked and began to reply, but I didn't hear what she said because my attention had been drawn to a familiar face at the bar. It took me a minute to place him, because he was out of context and obviously drunk.

It was Jake Carter, and he was staring in our direction. He blinked, nodded, and with a sudden jerky movement, he pushed away from the bar and began to make his way over with a shambling, unsteady gait. When he reached our table, he grabbed it to steady himself as he studied my face.

"I know you. You're the lawyer."

"Yes."

I stood up and shook his hand.

"Joth. Are you feeling all right, Mr. Carter?"

He glanced at Jenny.

"I'm good. Had a little too much, but I'm not driving."

"I'm glad to hear it. If you need a taxi . . ."

His attention had already drifted away from me and was focused on Jenny.

"I know you, too," he said.

Jenny pressed her cocktail glass on the tablecloth, making a ring of moisture.

"I think you're mistaken," she said quietly, without looking up.

"I know you. Jade."

"Jake, excuse me; her name is Jenny."

With a gentle smile, I took him by the elbow and turned him back toward the bar. Jake took an uncertain step, looked over his shoulder and submitted. Three or four steps later, I let him go and returned to the table.

"He's got a boat on F Dock," I said. "I hope he sleeps on it tonight."

Jenny forced a grin.

"How do you know him?"

"Friend of a friend."

"Everybody knows everybody around here," said Jade, not hiding her bitterness.

"Just a coincidence."

She picked up her drink and drained it.

"He's come in a few times. I'm surprised he remembers me."

"You're memorable, Jenny."

I smiled.

"It's the eyes."

"Nice try."

A new slant occurred to me.

"Does he come in alone?"

"He comes in with a guy."

A light seemed to go off and she looked up.

"Frank Racker. The guy whose card you found at my house."

"It's a small world."

I needed to move off that subject and quickly came up with a way to accomplish that.

"I enjoyed meeting your brother. He seems very polished."

"Polished. That's a good word. We're not close."

"Really?"

I paused, remembering something she had said.

"Lapsed Catholic? Is that why you've disappointed him?"

"I said, our relationship was disappointing. Maybe he disappointed *me*."

I shrugged.

"Most priests are disappointed in me, too."

"Just don't jump to any conclusions about him. Or me."

There was an edge in Jenny's voice I hadn't heard before. I wasn't sure how to respond.

"You'll be hearing from him. You can make up your own mind."

The food came. We talked some more. I tried to be funny, which is always a mistake for me. We skipped dessert and coffee. Carter was gone from the bar by the time we left and as I held the car door open for Jenny, I wondered if the cabin light I saw from F Dock was him.

Back at Del Ray, I parked in front of Jenny's house and asked her if she wanted me to come in.

"Not tonight," she said.

I got a peck on the cheek and cursed Jake Carter as I left her at the door.

Chapter Nine

Shopping for Clues

Before heading to Old Town the next day, I swung by Riding Time in response to Dan's request for a late morning cup of coffee. He had that rare ability to shake off legal and business risks like mosquito bites, but he looked concerned as he approached my booth, hands shoved deep into his pockets. As he sat down, I let him lead with some small talk until he came around to the reason for me being there.

"I need you to do me a favor, Joth."

I hated it when friends started with that.

"It wouldn't be the first time, Dan."

"I need to get rid of the kid."

" 'The kid?' "

"You know. I want to be fair to him, but it's complicated."

I nodded as the idea dawned on me.

"The kid being Chris. Okay, you mean you want to buy out Mama's interest?"

"Yeah."

"A little late for that, don't you think?"

"Maybe I made a mistake, but it still needs to get done."

"A little late is right. You had no authority to act for the company."

"I was the president."

"That's not what the corporate records say."

"How do you know?"

"Because they're in my office. You haven't had a meeting in seven years."

"We had a meeting, just before Mama's stroke. She hadn't been feeling well. Looking back, maybe we should have known."

"She owns half the stock, Dan. You can't do anything without her agreement."

"She made me president!"

Dan's voice boomed like a sudden squall and everything around us seemed to stop. People weren't used to Dan raising his voice. He looked around, folded his hands on the table, craned his neck, and recaptured his calm.

"Mama told me to take care of everything, which is what I did. What I did, I did for the best, you know, in her best interests."

"Chris is not going to deal with me."

"Of course, he is. You're the one person he *would* deal with."

Dan took a long breath.

"Look, he knows you're good. I've told him that, and he's seen you in action."

"And just exactly what is it you want?"

"I want you to represent him."

I laughed.

"Dan, you've finally surprised me. You want me to represent one client against another?"

"Look, Joth, you don't really represent me. I'm just a guy who sends you work once in a while. No conflict there."

"It's not gonna work."

"Besides, what if he hires somebody else? Then what happens? I hire you, and we get into a cluster fuck. Probably stuff comes out that doesn't help anybody, and everybody ends up worse. We need to keep the pie big, you know?"

I paused and turned it over in my mind. I knew from both training and experience that a lawyer had to trust in the structure of the law to deliver a just result. On the day we begin to substitute our own judgment, we put the law out of office and step on to a perilously slippery slope. But what Dan said made a certain amount of sense. There was plenty to fight about, and that made it appealing to lawyers who could churn the case or negotiate a substantial cut of the gross. The cash register would be ringing for the wrong people. Dan and Chris wanted none of that.

"Are you ready to make him an offer?"

"I can be. You can take it to him. You decide if it's fair."

"You think he's going to take your first offer? Or that I would?"

"Yes, I do, because it's going to be the right number. He doesn't want to dicker, and neither should you."

"But later on, he might feel like it wasn't fair, or it wasn't right; that I didn't protect him."

"Don't make me laugh. I'll keep paying his mom's medical bills 'til the day she dies. Like I always have. I'll pay him fifty thousand a year for ten years, no interest. Chris gives up all of her interest to me, and he stays away from the place."

Five hundred thousand seemed like a lot of money for a half-interest in a topless bar, but it was not a lot considering the properties Dan was rumored to own.

"Is Mama in anything else with you, besides the place?"

"Why?"

"You and she own a corporation. The place is owned by that corporation. What else does that corporation own?"

"What difference does it make?"

"Chris is going to have to give a knowing and intelligent release of his interest, or it's not going to be valid."

"You let me worry about that."

"He's gonna ask some question, maybe some questions you don't want to answer."

"Joth, he's a simple guy. He wants a living and for someone to take care of his mother. If you want information, just ask. If you have a right to it, you'll get it."

I believed him. Dan knew I'd keep the questionable stuff off the record, just like Chris would want it. His mother's name and money were as much at risk as Dan's. Still, something wasn't right.

"I don't like it, Dan."

"Since when does it matter if you like it? You'll be fixing it for me and fixing it for Chris. I thought that's what you do, Joth."

The means were questionable, but the goal was honorable.

"I'll need you to sign a waiver."

"Waive away."

"Let me think about it."

"Well, think fast. I should have done this years ago and I want to put the whole thing behind me."

"One more question. You know Jade's brother?"

"Father John?"

"That's the guy."

Dan's breath leaked out like air escaping a balloon.

"Sure, I know him."

"What do you know about him?"

"Why?"

"He wants to set up some sort of business arrangement with me."

I laughed.

"I guess the idea is that we refer sinners back and forth."

Dan looked at me with sad and weary eyes.

"Joth, you'd be smart to stay away from Father John."

"What?"

"He's looking for business, all right, but none of it's going to serve the Lord."

"What are you talking about?"

"Just be careful he doesn't get his hooks in you, because he doesn't let go."

Looking like he'd said too much, Dan folded his arms, which meant the shop was closed for the day. I got up to go.

"You gonna hang around till Jade comes on?"

I glanced at my watch.

"No. Tell her I said hi."

I never did get that cup of coffee.

***

I spent the next hour in a Starbucks, enough time to be sure that Jade was at work. Then I drove over to Del Ray, where I knocked on the door of her duplex.

"All right, all right!"

The young blond woman who answered the door was smoothing down her blouse, as if she'd just finished dressing. She looked to be about Jenny's age, with heavily made up eyes and a sour expression on a pretty face, marred by an unnatural pallor that the makeup couldn't hide. A sleeve of bright tattoos peeked out along her left wrist beneath her shirt cuff.

"Gala?"

"Do I know you?"

She sniffed and wiped her nose with the back of her wrist.

I summoned my most beguiling smile.

"Joth Proctor. Jenny's friend?"

"Oh yes," she said.

Her face brightened for a second and then clouded over.

"Is everything okay?"

"Oh, sure. It's just that I think I left my gloves when I was here last week. Brown leather with fur lining? Is Jenny home?"

She sniffed again and blinked her heavily lidded eyes.

"No, you just missed her."

"Oh. Well, I guess I could come back."

"I haven't seen any . . ."

"I think I left them on the sideboard."

She followed my glance toward the heavy, dark wood sideboard in the dinette, looked me up and down more carefully, and then pushed open the door.

"Let's take a quick look."

I followed her into the dinette. She moved a few things around, then looked up questioningly, wiping her nose again.

"I don't see them. Maybe Jade picked them up."

"I suppose it's possible. It wouldn't be such a big deal, being spring and all, but my sister, she got them for me when she was in Italy. They kind of mean a lot."

I picked up Track's card from where I'd left it.

"Oh, you know my buddy, Track!"

Gala leaned toward me to identify the card.

"Frank Racker?"

I chuckled.

"We call him Track. Everybody calls him Track because he's so big."

"He is a big guy. Kind of a teddy bear, really."

I put the card down and started toward the door.

"You seem awfully young to be buying a retirement vehicle."

She laughed.

"Frank says do it while you're young. It's cheaper then and you don't need to worry about it anymore."

"He's creative and always thinking ahead. Got to hand it to him for that. He was the first financial planner I knew to buy a viatical and spread the benefit around."

Gala giggled as if we were sharing a joke.

"Yeah. The guy's seventy and he's not going to live forever."

"Yeah, and he smokes. Well, nice meeting you and thanks for your help with the gloves. I'm sure I'll bump into you again."

***

The Bradford pears had bloomed overnight along the Parkway and I used the weather as an excuse to take the back roads south to Old Town Alexandria, knowing that afternoons as pristine as this were both brief and

140

infrequent. I drove slowly, soaking up the calming spring air.

Track had picked a neighborhood bar in the center of the ancient colonial port. I was punctual; he was early. He sat in a booth in the back corner, under an autographed photograph of the 1992 Redskins, nursing what looked like a gin and tonic.

"What kept you?"

I looked at my watch pointedly.

"Traffic."

"We got this done?"

The waitress who swung by was as grumpy as Track, and I followed his lead and ordered a bourbon and water.

"I'm not sure."

"Uh huh. How much is it going to cost me?"

"You don't miss much, do you?"

"Knott takes a big risk approving this deal, you know. He's not going to do that because I'm kind to animals, which I'm not."

I pinched my bottom lip and hunted for the right phrase.

"He wants a sweetener."

"You mean he wants more than just a free lunch."

"Yeah, and you don't seem surprised or upset."

"That seems to be the business he's in. News flash. I haven't got the money."

"Or is it a moral scruple that's troubling you?"

Track laughed at the concept.

"Like I said, I'm a businessman. There's other ways to approach it."

"Such as?"

He grinned savagely.

"Blow the whistle on him."

I shook my head.

"I thought you were smarter than that, Track. He gets pulled off the case and then what happens? Somebody else gets it; somebody tougher and more honest, maybe."

Track considered my point.

"I don't want that."

"Neither does he."

Track chewed a thumbnail and stared at me.

"You've done some digging, Joth. What did you find out?"

"For starters, I don't think this is the first time Knott's demanded a bribe. Or taken one, for that matter."

"How'd you find that out?"

I was hoping he'd ask.

"Some friends of yours over at Riding Time."

"Dan Crowley?"

"How well do you know Irish Dan?"

Track wagged his head inconclusively.

"I make it a point to know everyone who can help me."

"Anybody else over there I should know about?"

"Dan's the man. Everybody else is just hood orna-ments. What do you know about this guy? This Knott?"

"I know that mid-level state bureaucrats without family money don't send their kids to private school un-less they've got something extra-curricular going on."

Track raised his large, heavy hands.

"Perfect. We don't need to bribe him, Joth. And you won't turn him into his boss. But you'll threaten to go to that friend of yours in the Commonwealth Attorney's office."

My head snapped up and Track sensed that he'd hit a weak spot.

"Unless Knott approves my deal straight up."

I now saw all too clearly that I hadn't fully thought through how I might use the information Dan had turned up. I hadn't concerned myself with that part of what I was doing until I imagined Heather's face if she thought I'd stooped to extortion.

"You'll have to find somebody else to do that."

Track shook his head sadly.

143

"You're a piece of work, Joth. What have we been talking about since you sat down?"

I felt my face clench as Track nodded sagely. Getting in deep in like this didn't rattle him at all.

"He can't be allowed to get away with this, that's all."

"Do it yourself, Track."

He liked it when people pushed back. He smiled, almost kindly.

"I don't think I'm gonna have to."

He got up, threw a twenty on the table and strolled out.

***

An hour later, as I was thinking through my next steps on the Barkley buy-out, I heard the suite door open, followed by an exchange of voices. Mitch stuck his unshaven face inside my door.

"Someone here to see you, Joth."

Before I could step outside my office, I was greeted by the smiling face of Father John.

"I wonder if that offer of a cup of coffee is still available?"

I didn't remember making such an offer, but no matter.

"Don't see why not, if you can stand the stuff."

"We don't exactly serve gourmet at the rectory."

"I suppose not. How do you take it?"

"Cream and sugar."

I mixed it carefully while Irish Dan's ambiguous warning played in my head. Father John took the same seat he'd occupied last time and I put the cup on the table beside him. After a careful sip, he began his tale.

"I don't want to take up a lot of your time, Joth, but I do have a parishioner in trouble."

"Criminal trouble?"

"Yes."

"You didn't learn it in the confessional?"

He seemed appalled by the question, as I hoped he would.

"Of course not."

He put the cup down and assumed a meditative pose as he put his thoughts together.

"This woman is in her early forties. She's unmarried. I know her to be a fine, God-fearing individual. Member of the altar guild. But she's had some money problems."

"And she saw an opportunity?"

"Yes, she did."

"From her employer?"

He looked up at me with surprise.

"You've heard this all before, haven't you?"

"It's not the first time."

"She was the bookkeeper. At first, it was just a little bit here and there to tide her over, you understand. She'd put it back when she got paid."

I nodded.

"Sort of a bridge loan?" I said.

"Yes."

"Sure. Happens a lot. But it just proved too easy."

"That's right. I didn't know this was a pattern."

"I'm afraid it is. How much did she take in total?"

"Almost eight thousand dollars."

I whistled.

"That makes it a felony, Father. Do you have the paperwork?"

"No, she'll bring it in when she comes to see you."

"A big business?"

"No, small jewelry business. A cash business mostly."

That was an advantage. A cash business meant possible problems with proof.

"Court date?"

"I'm not sure. She knows. I hope you can help."

"What's her name?"

"Melanie. Melanie Freeman."

I wrote it down.

"Okay. You want me to call her?"

"Yes. Here's the number. And Joth, I was hoping we can work out some sort of discount? In light of the referral relationship?"

Now comes the kicker.

"You want me to do it at a reduced rate?"

"I was hoping."

If this was what Dan had warned me about, I could certainly live with it.

"Okay."

For a brief moment, I was grateful for Halftrack Racker and the enhanced hourly rate I was charging him.

"I charge $300 an hour. I can do it for $275."

He nodded gravely.

"Could you do it for any less? She's struggling, Joth, and money is tight in my business."

"What did you have in mind?"

"Even two-hundred and fifty, though well worth it, I'm sure, would strain our parish budget."

John saw me hesitate and smiled.

"Consider it a community service."

"All right, Father. Two-hundred and fifty an hour. One case at that rate and we'll see how it goes."

"I appreciate it, Joth, and so will Miss Freeman. Would it be possible for you to send the bills to the parish? We're going to help her out, of course."

"It's okay with me if it's okay with Miss Freeman. I'll let you know."

Chapter Ten

New Business

The predicted date for the peak bloom of the cherry blossoms was a week away. On that day, one of my favorites of the year, the Tidal Basin would be thick with tourists and locals, posing for the iconic DC selfie: young couples proposing marriage and senior citizens seeking the rejuvenating promise of spring. With the trees just budding, Jenny and I found a spot along Ohio Drive, where we spread a blanket on the soft, dry slope above the Potomac. Across the river, early season cyclists and joggers were out and about, and fifty yards from where we sat, Memorial Bridge transported its traffic of high finance, corruption and dealmaking in a nearly endless flow of commuters traveling at the pace of a funeral procession.

Jenny had called to say that she had something important to tell me and a look at the calendar reminded me what it was: the response date for nursing school admissions had passed, and I felt the sort of thrill that comes from anticipating a much desired yet unexpected gift.

She'd packaged some sandwiches, fruit and utensils in a soft-sided cooler, and I helped her spread the contents on the blanket. When I pulled out the bottle of champagne she had packed, I stopped and met her eyes. She smiled and handed me the PDF.

"UVA? I didn't know you were applying to Virginia."

"You never asked."

Jenny liked to cock her head. It was a mannerism that had already become beguiling. Her wry expression acknowledged a mutual awareness of an unspoken truth the two of us shared. By then, I owed it to her to acknowledge it.

"I underestimated you, Jenny."

"It's okay," she said with a wink.

I realized then it was more than that. I understood the thrill her phone call had caused in me. The subtle prejudice that had lodged deep within my Boston Brahmin bones had now dissipated.

She wasn't Jade the stripper anymore. She was Jenny the nurse.

Here was a woman who could withstand scrutiny on the fashionable North Shore of Massachusetts. I had been given much to start my life. I'd grown up in a 150-year old, federalist style home on the finest residential street in Salem, Massachusetts; I'd attended private schools from first grade through high school; I'd gone to an elite university on a lacrosse scholarship. My life was properly measured by what I had made of these gifts.

Jenny, by contrast, started with nothing. She'd worked her way into the same school I'd gone to through grit, discipline and hard work. I had settled into my place in life, but there was no cap on what she could accomplish. I admired her. I even envied her. Her achievements so far were more impressive than mine.

The news from UVA had cheered and relaxed her as well. She pulled an apple out of her basket and waved it.

"Just don't do it again," she said, with self-confident cheekiness.

I looked again at the PDF.

"UVA's nursing school is a two-year program."

She nodded.

"I got an associate degree from NOVA in December. "

"The community college?"

Jenny nodded again.

"I've been taking classes there all along. So, I'll go to Charlottesville in the fall as a junior."

"Third year. They call it third year down there."

She glowed.

"Yes, I understand they have a whole lot of quirky terms for things: Grounds instead of Campus, stuff like that. That's where you went, isn't it?"

"Yes."

"Well, you'll have four or five months to indoctrinate me."

"I guess I will. This sure is a cause for celebration."

I popped the cork of the champagne, and it released with enough power to reach the river.

"Do you think we should save it?"

"No, let it drift; a memorial to your old life."

She reached over impulsively and kissed me. In a quick minute, we were stretched out together on the blanket, the food and drink forgotten.

After a while, Jenny rolled away, folded her hands behind her head and contemplated the endless blue sky.

"Twenty-five; almost twenty-six. I'll be old for a junior."

"You'd be surprised. Nursing's a professional school. You'll meet a lot of people who have tried something else first."

"My old life is going to be dead and buried."

She turned her head and peeked at me.

"You thought I was older when you first met me, didn't you?"

My first instinct was to lie; my second was a resolve to give her only the truth. She deserved that at least.

"I'm not good with ages, Jenny."

"What *are* you good with?"

"My hands."

She laughed good-naturedly, and I let it go.

"I always enjoy visiting Charlottesville. It'll be nice to have a reason to go down there again."

"It's a date. By the way, did you find your gloves?"

It took me a second to recall the game I'd played to squeeze a little information out of Gala.

"Funny thing is, I had 'em all the time. They were in a different coat. I liked Gala, though."

Jenny took a crackling bite of the apple as she considered her response.

"Did you really?"

"I'm not sure," I said, keenly aware that I had already breached my commitment to absolute honesty.

"She seems like . . ."

Jenny held up a hand.

"She's a good roommate. She's got her issues, but she minds her own business."

"Is that her real name? Gala?"

Jenny giggled.

"No. She loves apples. Very particular about her apples, too."

"Looks like you've developed a taste for them yourself."

"Oh, yes. Never saw an apple I didn't crave," she said brightly, offering me a bite before playfully pulling it back.

"But I've already got a work name," she said, sounding glum.

"Jade. I like it. Green's your color."

"That name will soon be forgotten," she said. "Too many negative associations. I'll be glad when I've heard the last of it."

I nodded.

"Does everyone who works for Dan have a nickname?"

She thought about it.

"Pretty much. It's not the kind of work where you want people knowing your real name."

"And Gala?"

"She's a bartender. Bartenders have their own risks and opportunities."

"She'll miss you when you're gone."

"Oh, I doubt it. Dan will find her somebody else."

"Did he match the two of you up?"

"Yeah. Well, no. It's not like he gives a lot of thought to who will get along. It's just a matter of what's available when he hires you."

"So, all of his employees live in places Dan and Mama own?"

"Mama? Oh no, she's not involved anymore."

"She's not?"

"She had a stroke. Dan takes care of her."

"Is that why he lets her son hang around?"

Jenny made a sour expression.

"Chris was out of the area for a number of years. That's what I hear. Married some girl from Tidewater or something. Things didn't work out for him, so he came back here, and he's been trying to get back on his feet. We're supposed to be nice to him. It's supposed to be part of the job. No pressure or anything, but Dan always has a little extra at Christmas for those that do."

She put the apple down and reached out to take my hand.

"You know, I'll be so glad to get away from all that stuff."

"When do you think you'll be moving?"

"I don't know. I've got to get things tied up."

"Will you be looking for an apartment?"

Jenny's face tightened in a way that made her look younger. Or so it seemed.

"Oh, no. I'll be living in the nursing dorm. Can you imagine?"

I chuckled at the idea of Jenny living next door to a bunch of fresh-faced twenty-year-olds.

"You'll need someone to help you move down there."

"Are you volunteering?"

"Absolutely. I just might stay."

She reached over to hug my neck, and when I responded with a kiss, she jumped in without restraint.

***

On the way to work the following morning, anything seemed possible and a life that had eluded me until now appeared suddenly obtainable. I had no law partners, and I was on a month-to-month office lease. I owned my house, and it was a sellers' market. Housing prices were lower in Charlottesville, where I could just as easily hang up my shingle as in Arlington.

On top of all that, I'd be rid of Track Racker, who was beginning to make my skin crawl. That alone might be worth the move.

Melanie Freeman was on my schedule, and she was twenty minutes late. Perhaps it was her membership in the altar guild that predisposed me to expect a dowdy and unattractive spinster. I was surprised when she walked in. She was a remarkably striking woman, slim and still shapely, with rich hair that was graying into a luxurious platinum shade. She was dressed in a modest, violet pantsuit and her only jewelry was the silver chain and cross that hung around her slender neck, a discrete item, particularly when compared to the baroque monstrosity that adorned Tracks's mane of chest hair.

Like a former athlete, her self-conscious, stylized movements had slowed, but she retained the hints of her youthful grace. Only a complexion marred by too much sun, and perhaps too much rum, betrayed the hard miles she had endured.

"Thank you for taking the time to see me, Mr. Proctor."

She batted her eyes.

"I'm sure you're very busy."

"I understand from Father John that you've got a little trouble."

"Little is an understatement," she said, with a self-deprecating laugh.

She handed me the warrant.

"I can hardly sleep."

I sized it up quickly.

"Trademark Jewelers is your employer?"

"Was. He fired me."

Melanie had the habit of pausing between sentences to radiate an expression of admiration and trust. It had probably been an effective tactic ten or fifteen years earlier. She struck me as a woman who'd grown used to getting men to do her bidding and was now struggling to adapt to a new reality brought on by the inevitable march of time.

"How did he catch you?"

She sighed.

"I kept the accounts for years. He must have been suspicious because he had an outside accountant audit the books."

"Did he give you an opportunity to put it back?"

She shook her head vigorously.

"Just fired me and went to the police. He said he was very hurt."

"They usually are. It's not a great crime, relatively speaking, but it's a crime that stings. If they trusted you enough to handle the books, they tend to be personally offended. So, you didn't make any admissions? Any statements to the police?"

"I might have."

I looked up sharply.

"Might have what?"

"Might have said something to the police."

Her face clouded at my expression, like a child caught in an act of petty mischief.

"They had all the records."

"Did they read you your rights?"

"The Miranda thing? Yes, I think so. That I don't have to say anything?"

I nodded.

"It all happened so fast."

I picked up the warrant and studied it as a way to marshal my thoughts.

"It's hard to find a defense to these things. It's just numbers, and numbers don't lie. Eight thousand dollars is a lot of money. Can you pay it back?"

"I don't think so. I'm unemployed, after all."

"It would be better if you could. You'll have to make restitution as part of any plea agreement and if you could get ahead of the curve, it would help at sentencing."

Melanie's face fell as if she'd been arrested all over again.

I said, "Maybe you ought to see what Father John can do?"

"He's already helping out with my bill."

"I wanted to ask you about that. If it's all right with you, I'll send your bills directly to the church. I understand you'll contribute what you can. Is that correct?"

"Something like that. It's vague. But you won't say anything to Father John?"

"No, not a word about the case. My obligations run strictly to you as my client. He's just a source of payment. And that's okay with you?"

She nodded glumly. The full truth of her predicament was sinking in.

The preliminary hearing was set for the following week. I explained to her that at this stage, the Commonwealth was obliged only to prove that a crime had been committed in the county of Arlington and that she might reasonably be the perpetrator. If they met that low bar, it would go to the grand jury, where she would undoubtedly be indicted.

"The preliminary hearing usually presents an opportunity to explore a settlement."

"I hope so."

"You'd have to plead guilty to something."

She gasped.

"Really? There's no other way?"

"A lot depends on what you've already told the police. Let's see how the hearing goes. I can't predict anything more than that."

She stared at me, waiting for more. For a moment, I wondered if Father John had given her false hope, but then it occurred to me that she would have had no trouble generating false hopes on her own. That's what people in her situation usually do.

Chapter Eleven

Ethics 101

I'd tried to put Phil Knott out of my mind until I could find the time to come up with an appropriate approach.

He surprised me by calling first.

"I think we can settle your case," he said with a promptness that surprised me.

"I'm not sure. That sweetener you wanted . . ."

"Enough of that. I just thought differently about it. The government shouldn't be interfering with personal property."

"I see. Did you and Track have a little talk?"

He took this as an insult, which is how I intended it, and his tone hardened.

"I don't speak to represented parties."

"Sure. Sure. Wouldn't want to do anything unethical."

"You just make sure the department doesn't hear from Mrs. Moriarty anymore. If she's quiet, we're happy. And you tell your friend to back off."

"What friend? What are you talking about?"

"Never mind about that. I don't want to hear anything else related to this case from anyone. Understand?"

I understood that he'd been threatened and for the time being, it didn't matter who was behind it.

"What are you proposing?"

"Your offer seems fair. Mrs. Moriarty gets eight percent of the viatical by written contract between her and Racker, with $40,000 payable under the policy upon Carter's death from a covered event. No further financial obligation from her."

"That's it?"

There were a few other details, but they fell into place quickly and without controversy. So, I called Track.

"What did you say to Knott?"

"About what?"

"You know about what."

"What are you talking about?"

"Don't give me that."

"Joth, I don't know what you're talking about."

I had made a mistake. Track was a salesman, trained to bend the truth and adapt his story on the fly. It was not possible for me to judge his credibility over the phone. In frustration, I pushed it.

"You called him, Track. You threatened him."

"With what? With what you told me?"

"Yeah."

"And now you're threatening me?"

He paused and blew his breath out.

"If I didn't know you better, I'd think you were drinking. I haven't talked to Knott. I'm not going to talk to the guy. That's why I hired you. I don't know what you're hearing or from who, and I'm just going to pretend this conversation never took place."

With that, he hung up. I sat for a long while as I let the import of those two phone calls sink in. The idea of moving to Charlottesville was sounding better and better.

***

I had a lot to think about as I walked over to the courthouse. Heather was in, and I had barely settled myself in the reception area when I heard Betty call my name. She opened the door to let me in, and as Heather stood up from behind her desk to greet me her face fell.

"What's bothering you?"

"Is it that obvious?"

"I figured you came over to gloat about your little victory last week."

"Yeah, any excuse to drop by, but this is a bit more serious."

"I see that."

She shrugged, recapturing her world-weary insouciance and gestured toward the chair, as if I needed to be told where to sit.

She was wearing red, a magisterial scarlet, a color she favored on trial days. She thought it communicated an aggressive and combative attitude, and she was right. It also had the benefit of emphasizing her exquisite hair. As I sat, she used the opportunity to study me.

"Coffee?"

"Got anything stronger?"

She buzzed Betty and smiled as I turned my attention back to the problem I'd come to see her about. When faced with an ethical dilemma, it was my long-standing practice to consult Heather's sober but practical conscience.

After Betty brought my coffee, she began. "So, you have a problem. Criminal?"

"Ethical, maybe criminal."

"This isn't going to compromise anything my office is looking at?"

"As far as I know, the guy lives in Old Town. Anyway, anything he might have done happened outside your jurisdiction."

I had developed an explanation on the way over, but my thoughts had gotten jumbled in the elevator.

"I think a client of mine might have engaged in an act of extortion."

"Might have. Or did?"

"I don't have any facts. Just a hunch."

"Witness tampering?"

"No, nothing like that. A regulatory matter."

"This have anything to do with Dan Crowley's organization?"

"What makes you think that?"

"Because everything you do that's muddy comes from him."

"No, it's not Dan."

I scratched the back of my neck.

"Let's assume my client is an insurance broker who bought back a policy on his client's life."

"A viatical?"

"Exactly."

"That's a bit unusual."

"But not illegal. It does run afoul of state regulations, though. Or it might. Anyway, this client is being investigated by the State Corporation Commission."

I sipped my coffee and felt my way forward.

"In the course of my investigation, I learned a few troubling things about the SCC official who has the case. I'm afraid I revealed some of them to my client."

She frowned deeply, already visualizing the whole sorry transaction.

"How did you happen to do that?"

I stiffened.

"Casually and accidentally. Next thing I know, I get a call from the bureaucrat. He's dropping the case."

Heather placed a finger by her nose, a gesture I recognized as signaling deep thought. Then, she leaned forward and nodded judiciously.

"There are a dozen reasons why that might happen. Maybe he couldn't make the case."

"He was driving a pretty hard bargain a week ago."

"Have you confronted your client?"

"Yes. He denied it."

"So, all you have is a suspicion?"

"Instincts."

"Your instincts are usually good. What else do they tell you?"

"That I don't have enough to go on; that it's just a hunch."

"Did you raise your concern with the bureaucrat?"

"Yeah, he denied my client had talked to him. Of course, he's at risk, too. He doesn't want this stuff to get out, whether it's true or not."

"These 'troubling things' about the bureaucrat; this, uh, this threat; does it arise from professional conduct?"

"No, purely personal."

"Then you haven't got any obligation there."

"Right, and I've got my own obligation to represent my client zealously. About whom I have only a suspicion."

"I'd get out of the case, if I were you."

"The case is over."

"Well . . ."

She glanced out the window and the wheels continued to turn.

"You needed to confront him, but you've already done that. Beyond that, I think your hands are clean. Even if your client's are a little dirty."

"I just feel a little bad about it."

Heather nodded, and when she did, I felt as unburdened as a boy leaving Confession.

"You've always had a high standard on these things, Joth."

She moved some files across the top of her desk, and I reflected darkly on my recent conversations with Dan and Track. After a moment, I let the air ease out of my lungs and stood up.

"Looks like you had a trial today?"

"Yeah, statutory burglary. Not much to it, but I wanted the max sentence."

I nodded. I didn't feel up to the usual banter.

"Appreciate your time, Heather."

She stood up.

"Sure, Joth. You know where to find me."

Then she held up a hand to hold me for a moment.

"And Joth, one more thing. Stay away from Dan Crowley."

"I like Dan Crowley."

"Everybody likes Dan Crowley. That's the problem."

In the elevator on the way down, I acknowledged what I should have asked her: whether I could ethically represent both Chris Barkley and Dan Crowley in the buyout of Mama's interest in the business, but I already knew the answer to that. I didn't ask her because I was going to do it anyway. I'd need the cash to finance my move to Charlottesville.

***

I was back in the office when Chris Barkley called.

"Hello Mr. Proctor. Mr. Crowley said I should get in touch with you."

He sounded tentative and anxious.

"Call me Joth."

"It's about the business. He thinks it's about time he bought out my mom's interest. I could sure use the money."

"Anybody could use the money."

"He said you'd be fair with me."

"I'll give you the best deal Dan will let me give you, but you know Dan makes his own terms."

"He's always been fair to me."

"Is there a time you can come in? When we can meet and talk?"

"How about today?"

I glanced at my calendar.

"Today is fine. Three o'clock? Bring any paperwork you have."

I'd pegged him as anxious and ill at ease on the morning of Jenny's hearing, but most people are when awaiting trial. He was no better in my office. He was scrawny, with a pasty complexion and he wore a plain red necktie tied so tight it seemed to be constricting his breathing. The poor kid couldn't keep his eyes focused. Under his arm, he carried a file folder containing about half an inch of loose documents. I offered him coffee and he shook his head.

"No hard feelings about what happened with Jade," he said, with an unflinching generosity that impressed me. "I know you were just doing your job."

"Thanks. Appreciate it."

"I know. I was just . . . humiliated, I guess."

"Sorry about your testicle."

He shrugged.

"Well, I didn't lose it after all."

"No?"

"No, just swelled up on me. I was pretty upset."

I wondered if Sue Cranwell had known that when she demanded a guilty plea from Jade.

"Tell me about your mom, Chris."

"She's not doing well. She had the stroke five years ago this June, and she just kinda exists, if you know what I mean."

"She in a coma?"

"Coma," he said. "Coma. Yeah."

He repeated the word as if it came from a foreign language.

"Where is she?"

"In a nursing home in Del Ray. She was quite a lady, my mom. Came up from nothing. Made something of herself."

"Do you have siblings?"

"Did. A sister. She worked there, you know, at the place, but she died."

"I'm sorry."

"Drugs. I don't touch 'em anymore because of what happened to Jill."

"Father?"

"My dad, he's been out of the picture since we were little."

"And your mom's care? That must be expensive."

"Sure is. Dan takes care of it all."

"What's it cost per month?"

"Oh, I don't know. Dan takes care of it."

I swiveled my chair toward the window and thought for a minute. After a hard spring rain, the leaves of the maples along Wilson Boulevard were dripping.

"You know Chris, in this kind of deal, it's customary for both sides to have their own lawyer."

"Do you think I should have my own lawyer, Mr. Joth?"

"Proctor. Mr. Proctor. Or just Joth, if you don't mind."

"Dan has always been fair to me."

"How do you know?"

The question hit him with a force that was almost physical, as if I'd attacked his religion. He fumbled for an answer.

"He always did. I mean, he always treated my mom fair, even when she was healthy. She always taught me to trust Dan."

"I'm not trying to undercut your relationship with Dan. I just want you to think about it."

He shifted in his chair and loosened his tie, waiting for guidance from me.

"Why don't we see how it goes?" he said. "Would that be all right?"

"Sure."

I flipped open a legal pad as a sign that the preliminaries were over.

"Now, you understand that your mom actually owns the stock, so she's really my client, not you. Not exactly."

He nodded.

"You represent her interests because you hold her power of attorney."

"Yes."

"Did you bring it with you?"

Chris laid the file folder on the desk, opened it and leafed through check stubs, bills, tax returns and a clutter of miscellaneous material. The POA was a three-page document on redlined paper stapled to a blue backing. He passed it over and I read it through quickly. As I expected, it remained enforceable upon the signatory's disability. What I didn't expect was that the backup holder of the Power was Dante Crowley. "You're aware that if something happens to you, Dan becomes your mother's representative?"

"Uh-huh," he nodded. "I've offered to turn it over to him a couple of times. He thinks it's better this way, with me deciding."

"You've got some tax returns there?"

He had the returns for himself and his mom, but none for the business. The last three years had been collated and stapled as six individual documents, two for each year. I looked at his first. He had done part-time work, but the bulk of his income had come from the corporation: fifty thousand a year for miscellaneous services. This was generous, considering the only service I was aware of consisted of harassing the staff.

Fifty thousand a year was also the number Dan had offered to settle. I did some quick math while the kid watched. The returns and various health care bills showed that his mom got an annual distribution from the company in an amount equal to her medical bills and cost of care. This might also be generous, but there was no way to know.

"Do you have the company's tax returns?"

"No."

He seemed offended by the question.

"Why would I have those?"

"Because your mother is entitled to them."

"Never thought of that."

I scratched my chin.

"Chris, I've known Dan for years, and I agree he's a generous guy. But it's as if he told you you're entitled to half the jellybeans in the jar, but he won't show you the jar. When he tells you he'll give you a hundred jellybeans, you have no way to determine if that's half, do you?"

"I guess that's right."

"Let me make a suggestion. Let me talk to Dan. I'll figure out how big the jellybean jar is, then we can talk about dividing it up. Okay?"

"Okay."

"Give me a few days. In the meantime, just lay low."

"You mean, stay away from the place."

"I think that would be wise."

I got up and so did he.

"Mr. Joth, I wasn't sure about this. But now, I'm really glad I came to see you."

As we walked toward the door, Chris stuck out his hand, took mine and shook it awkwardly.

"Anything else you want to add?"

He thought for a moment, looking at his shoes.

"I'm happy for you and Jade. She's the only one of Dan's girls that doesn't do drugs. That's why I liked her."

I was startled.

"How did you know about Jade and me?"

"Dan."

"Dan talks too much."

"No. I just overheard him talking. I overhear a lot."

"Then, how come you know so little about the business?"

He cocked his head, as if this were the most serious question I had asked him.

"I've always paid attention to the wrong stuff. I'm just a simple guy, Mr. Joth. And I've got an ear for gossip."

Then he seemed to think of something else.

"You need to get Jade out of there, Mr. Joth."

"Out of the place?"

"No, away from Gala."

"Gala? I thought they were friends."

"She's poison, Mr. Joth. Don't you have a spare bedroom? A couch?"

I couldn't suppress a smile.

"I think I can do better than that, Chris."

It took him a moment.

"Really?"

I touched his shoulder in a gesture of assurance.

"Don't worry, Chris. We've already talked about it."

He nodded and winked at me.

"I'm glad. Jade will be, too. It'll be the best thing for her."

I nodded.

"Thanks again for seeing me today. I trust you, Mr. Joth, I really do."

I left my office soon after, hoping that Jenny would trust me that much, too.

Chapter Twelve

Working Both Sides

I picked up the phone to call Dan before something told me to stop. Instead, I swiveled toward my PC and Googled "retirement homes in Del Ray." There was only one. I checked for visiting hours, made a note of the address and got my coat.

Taunton Acres was a locally owned and operated facility situated in a converted warehouse not far from the river. The reception area was small, but clean and well appointed. Soft lighting on the exposed brick walls of the original construction lent a warmth and friendliness to the place. A low, wainscoted wall separated the reception area from a social room, featuring a TV, cabinet radio, and a couch and several chairs, arranged in a circle, facing a gas fireplace.

A resident was dozing in one of the chairs and a man who looked as if he couldn't have been a day over 85 played show tunes from his youth on an upright piano. An ancient woman in a wheelchair sat with her chin in hand and a distracted expression on her face.

In the reception area, a large oak desk faced the front door. Behind it, an elderly woman with a bun of gray hair and glasses, secured around her neck by a thin chain, worked busily at her paperwork. While I waited, I checked out the calendar of events on the bulletin board behind her. A flyer featured a grainy photocopied picture of my landlord in a Nehru-style shirt with bell sleeves, announcing, "Master Tran Instructs T'ai Chi," with a schedule of days and times.

I chuckled at this and the woman behind the desk looked up. She followed my eyes and smiled at me benignly.

"You've heard of Master Tran?"

"Actually, he's a friend of mine."

She turned again in her chair, studying the man in the photo.

"He's a fine man."

I took a moment before responding.

"Yes, he's a man of great subtlety and discretion."

"Is he now?" she said. "I'm Norma. Can I help you?"

I introduced myself with a name that wasn't exactly my own and asked about Christine Barkley. The woman removed her glasses and slid a well-chewed temple into her mouth.

"She hasn't had a visitor in quite some time," she said cheerfully.

"And I blame myself for that. I haven't seen her in years."

"Are you a relative?"

"No, business connection. Is there a chance I could see her?"

"I don't see why not. She's right there. Christine?"

Norma opened her hand in the direction of the woman in the wheelchair, who turned slowly at the sound of her name. I was so flustered that I forget the alias I had adopted and signed my own name in the guest book.

It was a chilly morning, and the gas fireplace warmed the little parlor. I walked over and pulled up one of the hardback chairs, as Christine Barkley regarded me with a blank look.

"Christine?"

Her once rich, dark hair had been reduced to a thin, unkempt fringe of white. She looked at me with a pair of light blue eyes that I remembered for their probing alertness. They'd dulled with the years and seemed vacant and unfocused.

"Christine? Mama?"

She reacted to the second name, which I assumed had become more familiar to her during the prime of her life. Her head barely moved, but her eyes took me in through a series of concentrated glances. Her gnarled fingers clutched a knitted blanket thrown across her knees.

"I know you."

"Yes, you do," I said, amazed. "I used to be your business lawyer."

"I can't find the name."

"Joth."

She did her best to raise a hand. She wanted a chance to dredge up the memory.

"Doctor Proctor."

Close enough. I nodded.

"It's been years."

"You still help at the restaurant?"

It came back to me that she used to refer to the club by that innocuous phrase.

"Sometimes I help Dan a little."

I slid the chair closer and folded my hands between my knees.

"But I'm here today to make sure you're okay."

"Who sent you?"

She'd been a big, robust woman with powerful arms and a personality to match, but age and illness had sapped her strength and reduced her to a frail shell. I was still getting used to how much she had deteriorated as I continued.

"Nobody sent me, Mama."

I remembered her son's statement that she was in a coma and my heart opened up to her. As far as I was concerned, it was an open question whether or not she was incompetent. Overriding my instinctive caution, I vowed to tell her the truth. It was Mama after all, who was my client, not Dan or Chris.

"Mama, I came here to tell you that Chris and Dan think it's time to work out a settlement. Dan wants to buy your interest in the business."

"They already did that."

"No, they didn't. You still own half of it."

"Dan's been taking care of me."

"How do you know that?"

The question may have been too much for her. Her eyes drifted away, and she seemed to shut down.

"He is taking care of you Mama. That's true. He pays all of your bills. Do you like it here?"

She looked around at the crowded bookshelves, colorful artwork and brightly painted walls but didn't seem to process much of it.

"I like it fine. They're good to me."

"Listen, Mama," I said slowly. "I'm going to talk to Dan. I'm going to make sure you have all you need. Is there anything you want to tell me?"

It was a foolish question, an insipid inquiry. She had no answer, and she was exhausted, but she had told me what I needed to know.

"I'll be back Mama, after I talk to Dan."

I stopped by the front desk and took my time signing out while Norma examined me critically, or perhaps she was just being protective of her residents.

"She's better than I thought she'd be."

"Is she?"

"Dan . . . Dan Crowley, he wanted a second pair of eyes looking at her. Anything I should report to him? Anything she needs?"

"Is your name really Joth Proctor? Or is it Rick Blaine?"

That was the name I first used when I walked in.

"Proctor."

I smiled like the kid with his hand in the cookie jar and made the best of it. I showed her my bar card.

"I don't know a lot of lawyers, but you're the first one I've met who operates under an alias."

There was a bit of a sparkle in her eyes as she said this. She seemed bored but curious, and I hoped she was ready to give me the benefit of the doubt.

"You know Dan Crowley?"

"I know he pays her bills."

"And you know her son, Chris?"

"I do, but not well."

"Mama . . . we all call her Mama, was Dan's business partner. Still is, as far as I can tell. Dan wants to buy her out. I'm just trying to make sure she gets a fair shake."

"Who's your client?"

"Chris wants to sell. Dan wants to buy. They both say they want to take care of Mama."

"You didn't answer my question."

I looked back at Mama and thought through my answer before speaking.

"If she's competent, it's Christine. If she's not, it's her son. Right now, I don't know the answer to that."

"You know you're the only person who's visited her since Christmas?"

"That surprises me."

"Does it?"

I shook my head.

"Not really."

Norma folded her hands and regarded me like a teacher evaluating a truant student's excuse. Then she opened a drawer and pulled out a file.

"Christine's a fine person and deserves better than this," she said.

She leafed through the papers and settled on a document, which she held up and studied before passing it to me.

"I'd fire an employee for doing this."

I looked around and then back at Norma, to assure her that no one was watching.

It was the Certification of Incompetence for Christine Barkley, which meant that Chris Barkley's power of attorney was in effect and he was authorized to make legal decisions for her.

"I understand that, and I appreciate it. I'm going to do what I can for her."

"Just keep me posted."

I smiled and told her I would.

***

By three p.m., the Riding Time lunch crowd had receded, and the happy hour regulars had not yet begun to trickle in. I announced myself at the bar and slid into an isolated booth. Dan appeared promptly and with a bigger smile than usual. I wondered if he knew where I had been. After the usual exchange of greetings, I told him, and he maintained his best poker face as he slid in across from me.

"How's she doing?"

"She's lonely."

He kept his gaze fixed on me as his expression moved from indignant to chagrined.

"I know she's lonely, Joth. Everyone in a place like that is lonely. You'll be, too, if you live long enough."

"She says you're taking care of her."

"That's right."

"We ought to be able to make the deal. I just need to know what she's entitled to."

"Yeah?"

"I need the business tax returns."

"I'm not giving you the tax returns."

"Why not?"

"They're proprietary."

"To her as much as to you."

"She's retired."

"I'll give you a confidentiality agreement."

"You don't need 'em. Look, Joth, who's your client? Me or the kid?"

"Consider it this way, Dan. If I don't get him something close to a fair deal, he's going to get his own lawyer. You know what'll happen then?"

"Whose idea was that?"

"I think it might have been mine. Chris has no idea what he's got because he's done a sloppy job as his mom's guardian, but I can't make the deal until I know what I need to know, which is everything."

He glowered.

"Look at it this way, Dan. Mama and Chris will release all claims on business entities you disclose. When she dies, Chris will inherit her interests in any business you don't disclose. I'm trying to give you a clean slate. You just better hope he doesn't hire a tougher lawyer than me."

"What do you want? How much better can she live?"

"You paid Chris a pittance of what he's entitled to and let him screw the help in return. That was the deal, wasn't it? Except that Jade wouldn't go along with it. That's what happened, isn't it?"

I paused and let the heat die down.

"I just need to make sure Mama gets what she's entitled to."

He looked away and rapped his knuckles on the booth table.

"All right. I'll get 'em to you."

"You want a confidentiality agreement?"

"You know I don't need that from you."

"There's something else I want."

"What a surprise."

He raised a hand and snapped his fingers and two cups of coffee appeared. I waited for the waitress to depart.

"I need some help with Phillip Knott."

"The guy I ran a background check on?"

"Yeah, that guy. I think someone's blackmailing him."

"What makes you think that?"

"He suddenly dropped the investigation of my client."

"Maybe your guy was clean."

I laughed at Dan's suggestion.

"What did you think would happen?"

"I wasn't sure, except that I didn't use the information you provided."

"You're losing me."

"Look at it this way. My client violated insurance regulations. Knott knew it, and he was acting on it for his own advantage. Then, he suddenly drops it about two days after I got your report."

"But you say you didn't use it."

"I didn't. But I think somebody else did."

"Why do you care?"

"Because I think it might have something to do with a client of mine."

Dan leaned back and scratched an eyebrow.

"And who's your client?"

"Frank Racker. You know him?"

"Halftrack Racker? Of course, I know him. He's more of a regular here than you are. You think he's blackmailing this Knott guy?"

"I hope not. He says he isn't."

"Then, what do you care?"

"Because if it comes back on me, I've got a problem."

This was a language Dan understood.

"What do you want me to do about it?"

"Let me worry about Track. I want you to tie down anybody in the chain; anybody who might have picked up any of the stuff you turned up about Knott."

"You got anybody in mind?"

"Anybody in the club who might have overheard. Anybody who's particularly nosy. Anybody who might be friendly with Track."

"You mean like Chris Barkley?"

"I was hoping you wouldn't say that."

"I run a strip club, Joth. I'm not saying some people here might not be capable of blackmail. But I am saying that these people keep to themselves and keep their mouths shut. Nobody wants their dirty linen aired. Chris is nosy; he might have been here when my source came in. He might have picked up something. Wouldn't be the first time. But he's not capable of blackmail."

"You sure about that?"

"He's not smart enough to pull it off."

I let that sink in.

"Let's get the buyout done first, Dan. We'll worry about this other thing after that. Okay?"

"Whatever you say, counselor."

"Jade around?"

I asked in a casual tone as I stood up. He looked at me carefully.

"No. She's been cutting back on her shifts. You know anything about that?"

I shook my head.

"No."

Since I didn't really know, I could honestly deny it, but I was thrilled to see that Jenny was already charting her new course.

Chapter Thirteen

Chris's Parachute

I was at my desk two days later, lost in thought, when a commotion in the lobby roused me. It was a courier with a package.

"Joth Proctor?"

I nodded. He asked me to sign for an inch of documents in a sealed mailing envelope. I took the package into my office and opened it on my desk. It contained a complete set of tax returns and backup financials, not only for Barkley and Crowley, Inc., but for three other limited liability companies holding commercial and residential real estate property in northern Virginia. Each of them was owned equally by Mama and Dan and they made a lot of money. But what both surprised and impressed me was what Dan had done with the money. Mama had gotten every bit of her half and more.

As I probed deeper, I understood why Dan didn't want me to see the books.

He had paid and booked the full cost of Mama's care as a business expense. He'd also written off a whole lot of his own personal costs, but not nearly as much as he paid on Mama's behalf. Because they shared what was left equally, Mama received a disproportionate benefit each year because her expenses were higher.

If the IRS got wind of Dan's methodology, it would mean a whole lot of trouble for him. This accounting was also dangerous for Chris. I appreciated that Dan trusted me enough to disclose all of this, but I wasn't sure I was happy about knowing.

Mama's personal tax returns were also included, prepared by the same corner-cutting CPA who had prepared the corporate returns. Chris, as Mama's power of attorney, had signed them, meaning he'd face personal liability if the IRS ever scrutinized the returns.

A by-the-book lawyer representing Chris would feel duty bound to call his client's attention to this chicanery, but after a few moments of thought I realized it wasn't that simple. Mama's care depended on this stratagem and on Dan's continuing largess. If Chris did things by the book, he would be stretched to find sufficient post-tax income to keep Mama comfortable. Any IRS investigation would not only put Chris in legal jeopardy; it would create enough financial chaos to literally be the death of Mama.

I picked up the phone and called Dan.

"Thanks for the tax returns."

"Surprised?"

"I was surprised by your generosity. I shouldn't have been."

"What are you going to do about it?"

"Keep it as simple as possible. $750,000 for Mama's interest in all four businesses. Two-fifty up front, with the balance at six percent over five years. Each party releases the other."

Dan took a moment to consider it.

"That seems pretty steep, Joth."

It was steep, but not by much.

"I think it's fair. You'll get Chris out of your hair. He'll be able to take care of his mother and have enough left to get his own life on track."

"Think he can manage that?"

"He's a big boy."

"What I mean is, what makes you think he'll use that money to take care of Mama?"

"You aren't suggesting that . . ."

"No, no. His intentions are good. He's just too dumb to manage it. Let's give him a chunk and put the rest of it in a trust for Mama. He gets what's left after Mama dies."

"Who'll be Mama's trustee?"

"You guessed it."

"I'm never going to be rid of you, am I?"

"Not if I can help it."

***

Chris came in the next day. A good lawyer, an honest lawyer, a lawyer protecting his own license would have told Chris about the questionable tax filings, about his risk and legal options, and about possible claims against Dan Crowley. But a sensible lawyer, a practical lawyer would recognize his client's limitations and just tell Chris what he needed to know.

That's what I did. I laid it out for him, backed by a tightly structured chart that I drew up for him as we talked. Then I sat back.

But Chris surprised me. He was craftier than I had given him credit for.

"I thought you'd want to talk to me about the tax filings."

"Okay. We could talk about that."

"But that would put Dan at risk."

"You, too. You'd end up spending half your inheritance fighting the IRS."

He nodded gravely.

"You know, I grew up around that bar. I hate to admit how much of what I know I learned there. I guess I just don't like the idea of being separated from it."

"It's not going any place."

"I know. But I am. I need to. I need a new start, you know?"

"Well, you'll have the money to do it, Chris, if you keep it simple and don't go overboard."

"I'm gonna buy a boat, go down to Florida and live on it. Do charters, fishing trips. Stay away from the nightlife."

"That's a good plan."

"How am I going to pay you?"

"That comes out of Dan's part."

"Well, I owe you."

"Okay."

I quickly turned the question of blackmail over in my mind again, the same one I had probed with Dan. Chris was leaving. There'd be no follow-up and he had no reason to deceive me. I just wanted to know.

"You know a guy named Frank Racker?"

"Sure, everybody around the place knows Frank Racker. "

"How's that?"

"Because Frank's the guy who supplies the girls with their drugs."

The rest of my inquiry quickly slipped out of my mind.

"Are you sure about that?"

"You're not going to say anything?"

"This is between you and me."

Chris nodded, looking as sober as a monk.

"He's the guy, Mr. Proctor. I don't think Dan knows it."

But he knew better than that. If Track was dealing drugs out of the place, Dan knew it and we both realized this. I stood up, thanked him and shook his hand.

"I'll have some documents for you to sign in a week or so. We'll be in touch."

We never got around to the question of blackmail or Phillip Knott.

Chapter Fourteen

Sue Cranwell Sweats

Sue Cranwell had the two o'clock preliminary hearing docket, and it was a long one. For a good prosecutor, it's assembly line work. Roll them out, one case after another. Call the complaining witness; call the officer; go through the checklist, putting on just enough evidence to show what's called probable cause, that a crime was likely committed within the court's jurisdiction, and that the defendant likely committed it. Prosecutors breathe a sigh of relief when a defendant appears unrepresented. The court will suggest the defendant obtain counsel and continue the case to another date, meaning one less problem for that day.

I had not entered my appearance in Melanie Freeman's case, and if Cranwell had scanned the docket that morning, she would probably have pegged Freeman as a breather, a chance to regather herself while the judge explained the facts of life to the accused. Instead, she heard my voice when the bailiff called the case.

"Defense is ready your honor."

I made my announcement as Melanie and I moved up to the counsel table just to the left of the podium.

Anne Gabriel had only been a judge since the first of the year. She'd never practiced law, but had parlayed a general counsel position with a Fortune 500 company into a seat in the general assembly, where her unimpressed colleagues offered her a judgeship as a means of getting her out of their hair.

"Call your first witness, Ms. Cranwell," she said.

"Commonwealth calls Nelson Taylor."

I made a complete pain in the ass of myself, which is not that difficult for me to do. Instead of granting the usual stipulations, I objected to everything, made Cranwell go through all the evidentiary hoops, and cross-examined with an aggressiveness that offended the complaining witness, forcing Cranwell to object.

"Your honor, Mr. Taylor's not on trial here."

That seemed to satisfy Mr. Taylor, who nodded smugly at me. It also satisfied Cranwell, who in all the confusion forgot to establish exactly where on Lee Highway Ms. Freeman had been employed. She made the same mistake with the investigating officer, who followed Taylor to the stand. Then, she rested her case and the judge asked if I had any evidence. I opted for a much different tactic.

"Defense moves to dismiss."

The judge sat back and folded her hands as my opponent moved to the edge of her chair.

"Mr. Proctor?"

"Your honor, Lee Highway is a long road. It runs through Arlington, through Falls Church and continues into Fairfax County. There's no evidence that this crime, if it took place at all, took place in Arlington, as the Commonwealth must prove as part of its case. I ask you to dismiss for lack of jurisdiction."

"Ms. Cranwell?"

She stood up, fumbling with her papers.

"The court can take judicial notice that Trademark Jewelers on Lee Highway is located in the 2700 block of Lee Highway, which is certainly within the County of Arlington."

When the judge turned toward me, I rose slowly to my feet.

"First of all, the court is not entitled to take judicial notice of the store's location. If it's true, it's a matter of evidence, and that evidence has not been presented. Second, if your Honor is inclined to take judicial notice of the location of a store in Arlington, you must also take judicial notice of another Trademark Jewelers in the 7600 block of Lee Highway. The 7600 block of Lee Highway is in Fairfax. The last time I looked, this court's jurisdiction does not extend to Fairfax County."

Cranwell tilted her head back in frustration.

"Your honor, the Commonwealth moves to reopen its evidence."

"Objection!"

"The Commonwealth's motion is denied," said the judge. "Anything else?"

With that proclamation, Melanie Freeman and I were back on the sidewalk a few minutes later.

"I don't even understand what happened," she said.

"I just bogged her down in technicalities."

"It was brilliant. Does this mean it's over?"

"Not necessarily. They can charge you again. And they probably will. I'll see if I can negotiate something."

Melanie exhaled with great relief, tossing wisps of her lustrous platinum hair off of her face, giving me a brief and unexpected sense of the vibrant young woman she had been not so long ago.

"Well, I've learned a hard lesson," she said. "I hope I don't have to learn anymore."

"And what would that lesson be?" I said, turning to face her.

"That it's not worth it, because you have to live with what you did, even if you don't get caught."

I wasn't sure I believed her. The lesson line sounded a bit too pat. But I knew one thing: the commission of a crime forces you to take stock of your life.

As I was trying to formulate a response, she placed her hands provocatively on her hips.

"Well, you'll have to let me make you dinner."

"I appreciate that," I said gently, "but I'm taken."

We made some small talk on the sidewalk and as she turned to walk away, I wondered where she was going. Probably the same place as me: home alone.

***

I got a call that afternoon from Father John. He was laughing, poking me to reveal details that were privileged between me and my client. I summoned the grace to put him off without telling him to go to Hell.

"You turned water into wine!"

This sounded like an oddly cynical comment coming from a priest, but I had heard worse, so I let it go.

"I guess Jenny had you pegged right."

"At least about some things, maybe."

"Send me your bill. I'll see that it gets paid right away."

***

I waited a day and called Heather. She didn't remember the case until she pulled it up on her computer.

I gave her a minute to find it and then I heard her grumble.

"You gonna recharge it?"

"Of course, we're gonna recharge it," she said, sounding cross.

"Will you give me a chance to talk you out of it?"

"You're wasting your time."

"What good's it gonna do, Heather? If she gets a conviction on her record, she becomes unemployable. She won't be able to make restitution, and she's likely to become a burden to the community."

"Has she got a job?"

"Not yet, but she's got a lot better chance to find one without this boondoggle hanging over her."

"You find someone to take a chance on her, and I'll talk to you about a misdemeanor plea. I'll give you two weeks."

***

I didn't feel comfortable closing Chris's deal without clearing it with Mama first. Chris held a valid power of attorney, so he was formally authorized to sell his mom's business interests on whatever terms he believed best, but I thought she should know about it, even if she lacked the capacity to fully grasp the intricacies or consequences.

It was a cold, dreary morning, which made this errand seem bleaker. But inside Taunton Acres, the warm, ambient light and the children's drawings of bunnies, eggs and springtime scenes lifted my spirits, as intended.

As I approached the reception desk, I heard the vague sound of a television at low volume and some whispered conversation. The same gray-haired, bespectacled woman was seated behind the reception desk, going through some paperwork while a radio provided a background of easy listening music. I remembered her. She was wearing the same dress.

"Norma, isn't it?"

She let her glasses drop so they hung suspended from a chain around her neck. "Yes, and what name are you using today?"

I couldn't help but laugh.

"I'm using my real name today, Joth Proctor."

"Here to see Christine?"

"I am. I was hoping late morning would be a good time to catch her."

"None better. She just had her breakfast and seems pretty sharp today."

I smiled.

"She's right there in the parlor."

I nodded my thanks and signed in.

The parlor was lined with books and painted in pastel colors. Mama was seated with her hands folded in her lap, staring at the glowing logs in the gas fireplace, as if they held the key to her future.

"Christine? Mama? Do you remember me? Joth Proctor?"

I squatted down beside her chair and let her focus on my face.

"Joth, isn't it?" she said, after a few moments.

"Yes, Joth Proctor."

She seemed to nod, then looked away and focused on a colorful child's drawing taped to the wall.

"Do you work for me?"

"Yes, I still do."

"How is business?"

"It's good. Dan and Chris are working hard. Do you miss it?"

"No."

She shook her head ruefully, as if she were feeling for the points of connection.

"Yes, I miss my girls."

"Well, a lot of your girls have moved on now, Mama. That's why I came to see you. Dan's offered to buy you out."

"He always wanted to buy me out."

"The price is good. It's fair. You'll have plenty, and so will Chris."

"What does Dan think?"

"He thinks it's a fair deal."

"And what do you think?"

I paused and reminded myself of the gravity of this question.

"I think it's a fair deal, too."

She dropped her head and looked at her hands, the bent fingers and deformed knuckles laced together.

"The girls will be taken care of?"

"Yes, they will."

"It will be good to sell."

"Then Chris and I are going to close the deal, okay?"

"All right.

She nodded.

It wasn't much of an affirmation, but it was enough because I understood that Mama knew she was getting out and that it was time. I patted her shoulder gently. "You'll be getting money, Mama. Is there anything else I can do for you?"

She took a deep breath.

"I'd like to go out for a drive."

"A drive?"

I stood up, wincing as I straightened my achy knees.

"Sure. I'll see what I can do."

I mentioned this request to Norma as I signed out.

"I couldn't release her to you, Mr. Proctor. I hope you understand. It would have to be Chris or Mr. Crowley."

"Well, let me see what I can do. Will you be here tomorrow?"

"Oh yes, we're a little shorthanded right now."

It took me a second, but then the light bulb went on. "Really? Looking for help?"

She rested her elbows on the desk and placed her chin on her folded hands.

"Yes, we are, but the right kind of people are hard to come by."

She looked up at me and offered a smile.

"There's no shortage of aging people in Northern Virginia, but our space is limited. It's hard to find good people at the salaries we can pay."

"And it's hard to know who to take a chance on."

"Oh, I don't know about that. I'm a pretty darn good judge of people. We're looking for good hearts."

"That's interesting, because I just happen to know somebody who might fill the bill for you."

"I'm listening."

"She's about 40," I said, fishing for the appropriate words, "and she's a people-person, you know, friendly and warm."

"A person like that could be a good addition."

"She's a little down on her luck."

I thought that comment might need some explaining.

"No, in fact it's worse than that. She's had a little run-in with the law."

"Oh dear."

"Yes, and it had to do with money. But I feel like she's learned a hard lesson, and she needs a second chance. Are you willing to talk to her?"

Norma looked at me closely as she thought about it.

"How do you know her?"

"I'm her lawyer."

I anticipated a polite but routine refusal, but she surprised me.

"I don't see why I couldn't talk to her. No promises, though."

"Who should she ask for when she comes by?"

"Me, Norma Tompkins. I'm the owner."

I gave her Melanie's name and told her I'd have her call.

"If she's serious, Mr. Proctor, have her come by. You can't tell much about a person over the phone."

I said I would and thanked her.

***

I called Dan on my way back to the office. I had to hold through two traffic lights before he came on.

"I need you to do yourself a favor, Dan."

"What kind of favor?"

"It's Mama. I just went to see her. If you want to get the deal done, you're going to have to sweeten it just a bit."

"Sweeten it? What the hell does that mean? I'm not going to renegotiate the terms."

"Relax. That's not the kind of sweetener I'm talking about. Tomorrow's going to be a gorgeous day. You pick her up after lunch and take her for a drive. Go down the Parkway to Mount Vernon and back. And make sure you stop and get her some ice cream."

"Have you lost your mind?"

"Those are the terms, Dan."

"Mama said that?"

"No, I said that. She made you rich. Maybe you made her rich, too, but that's what she deserves."

I heard him exhale.

"Joth, I've got a busy day tomorrow."

"Come on Dan, you're a big deal in this town. Make time, and as soon as Mama tells me what kind of ice cream she had, I'll get Chris to sign off.

***

Back behind my desk, I called Melanie Freeman, who seemed happier to hear from me than I expected, and her enthusiasm filled me with a surprising warmth.

"Are you having second thoughts about that dinner?"

"No, but I ran across an opportunity you might be interested in."

I briefly explained the situation at Taunton Acres and suggested she make arrangements to meet with Norma Tompkins.

"You're going to have to come very clean with her about your last job, but Ms. Tompkins is in the business of helping people, and I think that's something you could be good at, too."

Melanie thanked me profusely.

"I've been finding out that a mistake like the one I made has legs."

A vision of her still-shapely legs passed quickly through my mind.

"All you need is another chance."

I hung up the phone and walked up the wooden stairs to DP Tran's low-ceilinged lair on the second floor, intending to cash in on the favor he owed me. He was seated in his private office behind an ornate desk, staring owlishly at an oversized computer monitor, which looked like a relic from the prior century.

As soon as I knocked, DP swiveled away from the monitor and folded his arms across his wiry chest.

"How come you don't refer me work?" he said.

I recognized the familiar arch in one of his expressive eyebrows.

"None of my clients have needed bail bonds recently."

I peeked over his shoulder. He had been studying a spreadsheet that may have been his business ledger. I couldn't make out the numbers, but several of them were red.

"Be patient."

"I mean goddamn detective work."

"Because your license was revoked."

"I don't need a fucking license to follow a car."

"You do if you want to get paid for it."

"It's because you do it yourself."

I took a seat. That was true.

"I enjoy it."

"You bastard, I send you all my legal work."

"You want me to send you a bill for squeezing the rent out of Mitch?"

He sneered.

"You think you're a better investigator than me."

"There is something I want you to do."

Those expressive eyebrows bobbed, and he rubbed his tiny hands.

"It's not detective work exactly, but it pays like it," I said, wondering how I backed myself into these situations.

DP's eyes narrowed. He was always suspicious of me, and for good reason.

"What kind of work?"

"I need you to speak to Norma Tompkins."

"I don't know who you mean."

"At the place where you teach T'ai Chi to the old ladies and kooks."

He looked around like a weasel, seeking an escape route.

"Don't worry. Your secret's safe with me. I've got a client trying to land a job there and I want you to put in a good word for her with the boss."

"Who is this person?"

"Her name is Melanie Freeman. I'll tell you all about her."

And that's what I did. That's how it was with DP and me. We traded favors like kids trading baseball cards. Somehow, I always got the cards with the bent corners, but DP was much like Dan. He trusted me, and that quality was both rare and irreplaceable.

Chapter Fifteen

The Drowned Man

Track called me at the office.

"Jake Carter's dead."

"What?"   .

He sounded spooked and nothing spooked Track Racker.

I bounced out of my chair.

"What happened?"

"He drowned."

"What do you mean he drowned?"

"Somebody found his body this morning underneath F Dock."

I walked as close to the window as the phone cord would allow. It was an otherwise calm day. The trees along Wilson remained still on a windless afternoon, but I felt turbulence heading my way like a squall.

"How'd you find out about it?"

"His wife called me last night, looking for him. I drove over there this morning to see if he'd turned up."

"Where? The marina?"

"No, Carter's house. Maureen told me."

"What time was that?"

"I don't know. Early. Before the police came."

Jake Carter dead!

I sat down again.

I thought of Jake as the sort of likeable, easygoing guy who lets things come to him and drowning as a fate for the careless or reckless. We needed more people like Jake and now we had one less.

"I'm sorry to hear that, Track."

"There's one more thing. The police want to see me. Is that a problem?"

"It's always a problem when the police want to see you. Did they say why?"

"They said it was routine."

Nothing was routine when somebody was dead.

"What did you tell them?"

"I said I had a crowded day and that I'd call them back."

"Smart. You'd better come in."

He didn't ask why.

"How 'bout right now?"

"Works for me."

***

It was just before two when Track called, and I fig-ured I'd see him within the hour. I'd almost given up on him and closed the office for the day when he finally showed up. I heard the outside door open and met him in the reception area.

"What kept you?"

He pulled on his chin.

"The cops got impatient."

"They came by?"

He jammed his hands deeply into his pockets and sighed.

"Yup."

Daingerfield Island was federal jurisdiction.

"DC police?"

"No, Alexandria cops."

I ran a hand through my mop of graying hair.

"You want some coffee?"

"Water."

He looked around.

"If you have it."

I found a bottle in the mini fridge inside Mitch's empty office and poured a cup of stale coffee for myself. Then I led Track into my office and shut the door.

"Did they read you your rights?"

"That's the first thing you're gonna ask me?"

"Well?"

"No, they didn't."

"That's a good thing."

I settled back behind my desk.

"DC's farmed out the basic groundwork to the locals. They're just doing their homework. You know, they want to see if it was an accident, a suicide, or whatever."

"You're making me nervous. What's the whatever?"

If Track was nervous, he didn't show it. I remembered the way he fidgeted on the morning he first introduced me to this problem. Now, he was as alert and attentive as a well-qualified man at a second job interview.

"Do they know about the viatical?"

"It didn't come up. Why would that matter?"

I sipped my coffee."

"Might matter if they thought he was killed."

"He wasn't killed. He slipped and hit his head."

"Did they tell you that?"

"No."

He crossed a leg over his knee, and it began to jiggle.

"I'm just . . . look, what are you talking about? No one says he was killed."

"Listen, a guy's dead in what might look like suspicious circumstances. You've got an insurance policy on his life, Track. That means you've got a motive. That's what they look for."

"A motive for what?"

I didn't say anything because he knew the answer.

His chin tilted up and he shut his eyes for a long moment so that when he opened them up again, he was looking at the ceiling.

"Hadn't thought about that."

"So, what did the police want to know?"

"When I last saw him."

"When was that?"

"I don't know. A couple of days ago. He doesn't have a lot of friends, and I drop by to visit at the marina every once in a while."

"They ask anything else?"

"If he had any substance problems, was depressed, having any trouble at home, you know."

"What did you tell them?"

"That was hard."

He folded his hands together and turned the cradle formed by his fingers toward his face, as if he had written a note to himself there.

"Jake and his wife didn't get along. But I didn't want to get in the middle of that."

"What did you tell the police?"

"Yeah, okay, I told them that Jake and Maureen were lovey-dovey."

"Okay. Did they tell you how he died?"

"They just said that he drowned. I guess that's the logical deduction when someone is found face down in the Potomac."

I gave it a moment's thought.

"Okay, nothing else to do right now. Just don't talk to anybody, especially the police. We'll just have to wait for the coroner's report."

I got up and so did he.

"You know anybody on the D.C. police?" Track said.

"I'm not sure," I said, but I did.

"By the way," he said, turning back to me with his hand on the doorknob, "about your money. I'll have the other three thousand to you next week."

I saw his eyes narrow in response to something he saw in my expression.

"What's the problem, Joth? I told you you'd get paid."

Chapter Sixteen

Questions on the Waterfront

Metro Police have a substation on the Southwest waterfront, just around the corner from Fort McNair, where they hung John Wilkes Booth's co-conspirators in 1865. A lot of people feel that police work in D.C. hasn't improved since then, and the guy I knew was in no hurry to change that perception.

The Southwest substation was staffed with officers who had boating experience and anti-terrorism training. There's not a lot of conventional crime along the river, and over time, day-to-day investigative skills have eroded.

Mark Franklin was a traditional cop from a legacy cop family in New Jersey who happened to have grown up around boats. He was known to go easy on boaters who let the deadlines on safety equipment and registration slip, so he had a reputation as a pushover. I'd met him when I represented a bit player in a cocaine smuggling case several years before. My guy talked and walked, and everybody was happy, except the kingpins doing serious time.

I made sure Mark was on duty, then showed up in Southwest, where redevelopment of the waterfront was in high gear. Mark was a stocky man who'd been a wrestler in college, and he still looked like one. He was in a typically good mood.

"Let's step outside and get some air," he said.

We found a park bench along the boulevard and took a seat where we could enjoy the breeze and look across at Hains Point and beyond it, Reagan National Airport on the Virginia side of the river. I told him I represented Frank Racker and was just doing my due diligence.

Mark peeked at me with piercing blue eyes.

"I'm surprised he thought he needed a lawyer."

"I represent him on some minor regulatory issues."

"And you're just curious."

"Naturally."

Franklin laughed. He was a guy who liked to laugh in a job that gave him little opportunity. My edge was that I knew that about him.

"Doesn't look like there was much to it," he said, "as far as we can tell."

"Had he been drinking?" I said.

"You can't wait a week for the report?"

"You know me, I'm impatient."

"And curious. Carter left the bar at about ten. Died between then and midnight, most likely."

219

"You're painting a pretty clear picture."

"Probably. You know anything about him?"

"I was over there last week, and he was hitting the rum pretty hard."

Franklin's eyebrows shot up, and he studied the backs of his hands.

"What were you doing over there, Joth?"

"They've got a nice restaurant."

"You gonna tell me you had a date?"

"Does that defy belief?"

"No. I just thought . . . well, whatever. You know anybody on F Dock?"

"One less person now."

"Yeah, you want his slip?"

"Does the boat come with it?"

"That's a hell of a nice sailboat. And you know what? The guy never took it out."

"So, what happened? Passed out and fell in?"

"No. His bedroll was laid out in the cabin. Looked like he'd been in it. My guess is, he got up to go take a leak, missed a step, fell and hit his head on the dock. We found a little bit of blood."

"Fall kill him?"

"No, probably knocked him out. He got wedged under the dock and drowned. But that's just what I think."

"Bad luck."

"Yeah. Okay, now tell me what you know, Joth."

I laughed. Franklin was a rare cop, a straight shooter who'd tell you what he could first, without exacting any promises, but he expected reciprocity. Usually I'd comply, but I couldn't put my client in the crosshairs. Not this time.

"Not much I can tell you, Mark."

"How's Racker involved in this?"

"I'm just putting my foot in the water."

"Like maybe he's having an affair with Carter's wife?"

"What?"

He was watching me like a hawk.

He nodded.

"Just a rumor."

"You better be careful where you spread that."

"Just wanted your reaction."

"Well, you got it. Does that explain why the police wanted to question him?"

"Far as I know, that was just background."

The wind had picked up. I pushed my hands back through my hair.

"Well, thanks, Mark; you've given me a lot to think about."

"Let me know where those thoughts lead. If you can."

***

The next day, I was at my desk, studying UVA's lacrosse schedule, when the phone rang. It was Marie's day off, so I picked it up.

It was Heather. She made a few minutes of small talk before working her way around to asking me to meet her for a cup of coffee.

"What's up?"

"Nothing's up," she insisted, in a way that assured me that something was.

"Don't you have someone you need to put in jail?"

"I had a trial this morning, but it pled. I'm not due back in court 'til two."

"Okay. What do you have in mind?"

She named Willard's, a coffee shack off the beaten track that was usually quiet after the cyclists left for their morning ride. It was the kind of dreary early spring day that could put a chill in your bones, but it wasn't raining. I always said it would be a rainy day when I turned down coffee with Heather. We agreed to meet in fifteen minutes.

When I got there, she was at a corner table, facing the door. She stood up when she saw me, showing off a well-tailored red pantsuit, her battledress. She had a steaming cup of tea in front of her. I sat down and ordered the same.

"I heard that somebody drowned over at the Washington Sailing Marina a couple days ago."

I looked at her carefully, and she returned the stare, her lovely face betraying nothing.

"That's federal jurisdiction. Outside your bailiwick."

"Doesn't mean I can't be curious."

I steepled my fingers and studied her, then considered the place she'd chosen for this meeting.

"Isn't this where you take reluctant witnesses to work them over?"

"Sometimes. How'd you hear about it?"

"Hear about what?"

"Don't be cute with me, Joth. Why do you think I'm asking?"

I thought about it and blew out my breath.

"That's a good question."

"We've known each other a long time. I know you're an ethical guy, but sometimes . . ."

She fumbled for a word and Heather never fumbled for words. Or maybe she knew what she wanted to say but was having trouble finding words she was willing to employ. So, I helped her.

"Except sometimes I shoot from the hip a little."

"Not just a little. So, how did you know Jake Carter?"

"What makes you think I knew Jake Carter?"

"Didn't you tell a cop that you did?"

I sipped the hot tea and warmed my hands on the outside of the cup as I let my mind run backward. She was right. When I thought I'd been squeezing Mark Franklin for free information, I had told him that I'd seen Carter drunk in the marina bar, which meant I recognized him and that I'd seen him before. I could have kicked myself for that slip, but instead I nodded at Heather and instinctively adopted my best poker face.

"Sure, I met him. Due diligence."

"Did you recognize him in the bar, or did you go looking for him?"

"What are you talking about?"

"The law enforcement community is small, Joth. You know that. Someone's eventually going to ask you these questions. Might as well be me."

"I had a date at Indigo Landing."

"You must like her."

"I do."

"Glad to hear it. How'd you happen to know him?"

"Friend of a friend."

"You aren't getting paid out of the viatical, are you?"

"Are you asking me as my friend, as a prosecutor, or as my legal advisor?"

"Just putting the pieces together. It's what I do."

"Except you get to pick the puzzles you work on."

She threw her head back and shut her eyes.

"I don't like the choice you're giving me any more than you like the questions. All right, Joth, let's see . . ."

She took a long sip of tea and I watched her work through the factors in her head.

"Guy dies outside my jurisdiction, but I'm an officer of the court. The police ask me some challenging questions, not in my capacity as a prosecutor, but as somebody acquainted with you. I've regularly provided you ethical advice in the past, and it's always been under the attorney-client protection. Okay, as your lawyer. Consider this a protected communication."

She didn't much like it, but she assumed I had an honest motive and she'd known me too long to back away from me now.

"Okay, Heather, so what's going on?"

"What do you know about Carter's death?"

"Not much. Just what my client told me."

"Do you have reason to believe a crime has been committed?"

"No. As far as I know, it was an accident."

"But you weren't there?"

I leaned forward and folded my hands between my knees.

"Okay. A guy dies. My client has a life insurance policy on him. But you already know that."

"You have to admit that's unusual."

"But it's not illegal."

"The guy with the policy, he's got a motive."

"Maybe. Probably."

I wagged my head.

"Yes. Let's assume he hired me to look into the legality of the viatical."

"And you advised him."

"I didn't advise him anything. You hit on the problem. He told me I'd get paid next week, so yeah, that means he's paying me out of the proceeds of the policy."

She blew her breath out.

"So, you've got a motive, too."

"I don't know. Do I?"

Heather's expression saddened as she looked at me, as if she didn't understand how I could be dumb enough to get myself into this predicament. I didn't understand it either.

"Do you have any reason to think your client would . . ."

"No."

"He hasn't said anything?"

"No."

"Well . . ."

She stared out the window and spoke as she thought it through.

"The police don't believe there's been any foul play, as far as we know. Your client benefits from somebody else's death. That happens."

"Yeah, but so do I. That doesn't happen every day."

"You can take the money, if that's your question. It's not an ethical problem. Of course, if you do and if things change, you might have some tough questions to answer. And one other thing Joth. You better be the first person to figure out what happened."

"Does Franklin know about the viatical?"

"I don't know. I don't think so, but if he's doing his job, he soon will."

"Maybe."

I knew Mark Franklin well enough to know that he might not. I also knew that Heather was right. I needed to get this worked out before he did.

"All right, Heather, thanks for the advice."

I let her pay for the tea.

Back at the office there was a message on the answering machine. I heard Melanie Freeman's silky voice, thanking me for introducing her to Norma Tompkins. This was just the breath of fresh air I needed.

"I appreciate it," she said, "and Father John's right. You're worth every bit of $300 an hour."

There was no need to call Melanie back and she hadn't even left a number. Something that Track said had been swimming around in my mind: Track was in the habit of visiting F Dock, but it was a secured location. I picked up the handset and called him. He was at home and picked up right away. I told him most of the truth, that I'd just talked to my friend at the Metro police and that I needed to see him immediately. I didn't mention Carter's wife. He tried to beg off.

"Now, Track. Right away."

I played my hunch.

"And one more thing. I want the other fob."

"What fob?"

"The fob you used to get on to F Dock. You know what I'm talking about. Bring it over today. Before somebody else asks you for it."

***

I had some things to do until mid-afternoon. When I got back to the office, Track was waiting for me, looking surlier and more combative than usual. I grinned at him.

"That was prompt."

He wasn't amused. I led him into my office and closed the door.

"You got the fob?"

He pulled it out of his pocket and tossed it across my desk with a display of animus that caused it to bounce onto the floor.

"Anybody know you have this?"

"Just Mo . . . Maureen, I mean."

"It would be better for you if you forgot you did."

"How'd you know?"

I picked it up without comment.

"I'm a good guesser. I hope nobody else is."

You didn't beat around the bush with a guy like Track.

"My guy at the Metro police says you're having an affair with Carter's wife."

He studied me, measuring me, then nodded his head.

"Thinks or knows?"

"If he thinks it, Track, he's gonna know it soon."

He rubbed his jaw and studied the lighthouse picture on the wall.

"We were friendly, yeah. Still are."

"How friendly?"

"Friendly enough to be careful."

"Did Carter know?"

"Probably. He didn't care. He spent as much time on the boat as possible."

"Is that cause or effect?"

"Look, Joth, I stopped by their house that night. She'd been worried about him. I was driving by and I wanted to see if he'd come home."

"Were you still there the next morning when the cops came by?"

"No, no, no; I'd already gone."

"Then how did they know about you and Maureen?"

"They asked her if anybody could account for where she was when her husband died. She told them I had dropped by. I had to back her up."

"Are you in the habit of dropping by?"

"In the evenings, yeah. That's when Jake and I usually did business. I didn't know he wasn't going to be there."

"So, you're her alibi. And she's yours."

Track looked at me blankly.

"That's awfully convenient, isn't it?"

"I don't think they've got anything, Joth, except rumors."

"What kind of rumors?"

"I don't know."

"Those are the dangerous kind, Track. When the cops interviewed you, did this come up?"

He rubbed his hand together, then ran them down the sides of his nose.

"I'm not sure. The questions touched on it, but they were general, like 'how well do you know the family' and that sort of thing. I was careful not to lie."

"But you confirmed her alibi."

"It's the truth," he said. "What else am I going to say?"

"Good policy, but you're not talking to them again."

"Lawyer's orders?"

"Absolutely."

"Anything else?"

"Yeah, did you kill Carter?"

"Are you kidding?"

"I just want to hear you answer the question. Because I'm going to be answering it soon myself."

"I didn't kill Jake Carter."

He was firm and didn't flinch, just as I hoped.

Chapter Seventeen

Outdoor Sports

The marina chandlery on Daingerfield Island was brightened by windows overlooking the water on two sides. The shelves along the back wall featured branded clothing, nautical knickknacks, and basic sailing supplies. Nobody from this marina was sailing to Europe any time soon, but all the patrons could dress as if they were ready to embark. The young man behind the counter wore a Washington Nationals T-shirt and Bermuda shorts. He didn't look up as I approached, watching the glow of the computer screen playing on his unlined face.

"Is this where I ask about renting a slip?"

He tilted his head in my direction to look me over. In jeans and a yellow slicker, I looked like a reasonable approximation of a yachty type.

"You want a slip?'

"Is there something wrong with your hearing?"

He pushed away from the computer and stood up.

"Sorry, I misunderstood."

"If one's available at the right price, yes."

He adjusted his dark framed glasses.

"What kind of boat do you have?"

"It's a Hunter 19," I said, identifying the make and length of a vessel that once belonged to a friend.

"I'm getting a pretty good deal, but I'm not going to close on it until I know I've got a place to put it."

"Sure, we could find a place for a boat like that."

"What's the price?"

"Well, let's see. Nineteen feet."

He did a quick calculation and quoted a price that was substantially more than I paid for my first car.

I nodded and looked at him probingly.

"How's the security around here? I understand somebody just got killed?'

"Oh, no. The gentleman fell. He was working on his boat. We discourage that sort of thing around here."

"Liveaboards?"

"No liveaboards. We have a strict rule about that. We don't allow slip holders to sleep on their boats."

"Liveaboards!" I said. "God bless 'em, but nothing harms the quality of a marina like liveaboards. One step up from vagrancy."

"Couldn't agree more."

"So, you have twenty-four-hour security walking the docks?"

"Well, we don't find that we need that here. This here is federal property, and we put a premium on privacy."

"Fair enough. I think we can work something out."

"Do you want us to draw up a contract?"

"I assume you've got a standard form?"

"Of course."

I held my hand out.

"Let's have it. I'll show it to my lawyer."

"We don't negotiate."

"You haven't met my lawyer."

He gave me a copy, and I left.

***

The mist had burned off by the time I arrived the next morning. Scents of brackish water, fresh cut lumber and the fumes of outboard motors mingled in the morning air. I observed several mariners already up and about; early risers adjusting lines and tightening fittings on adjacent docks.

The only person visible on F Dock was polishing the brightwork on a sloop, tied up near the end of the dock. Across from him was a vacant slip. I opened the F Dock gate with Track's fob and walked purposefully past the *Southern Patriot*, giving the remnant of yellow police tape a curious once-over as I passed. I made a show of inspecting the empty slip, visually measuring the width of the bay, the condition of the finger-like ramp. Then, I checked out the sloop berthed in the adjacent slip. I dawdled until I caught the attention of the sailor at work on his fittings, then turned to look at him quizzically. He was a slim, fit, African American with a neatly trimmed beard.

"Looks like you lost something."

I forced a bemused grin.

"Not yet. I'm thinking about losing about $1,300 dollars on this slip and wondering if it's a good idea."

"Really?"

He got to his feet, stretched his lower back and jumped down to the dock wearing the ready smile of a man with an instinct to defuse potential confrontations. He struck me as so tense and high-strung that for a moment I wondered if it was really his boat.

"Name's Charlestraton."

He extended his hand.

"Lincoln Charlestraton."

"Victor Lazlo."

I shook his outstretched hand.

"They call me Vic."

"Vic. Vic. Nice to meet you, Vic. Call me Linc."

"How long have you had this slip?"

I gave his boat a quick scan.

"Four years."

I prodded the utility stanchion at the head of Charlestraton's slip with my toe.

"Electricity, running water, everything certainly seems well maintained."

He chuckled.

"The federal government takes good care of its sailors."

I jerked my chin over my shoulder.

"What happened there?"

His face clouded.

"Unfortunate thing. Poor guy took a fall."

"Hope he wasn't badly hurt, but it looks like he was."

"Killed him, I'm afraid. Jake Carter. One of the nice guys."

"No!"

"Yeah. Hit his head and drowned."

"How did that happen?"

Charlestraton scratched beneath his Orioles cap and glanced about him.

"Tell you the truth, I think Jake might have been drinking. Wouldn't be the first time."

"Liveaboard?"

"Well, they don't allow liveaboards here, but for Jake, they were a little less than vigilant. Nice guy, and nobody wanted him driving at night."

"I see. So, he got up to go to the head and . . ."

"I don't know what got him up. He kept a pretty low profile."

"Woman, probably."

"Nah, not Jake. I've only known one other person to visit him."

I had almost everything I needed.

"Big burly guy with a beard?"

"Yeah."

Charlestraton cocked his head and eyed me suspiciously.

"Fella like that used to come by sometimes. You can't miss him."

I grinned at him. No, you can't. No wonder the police got on to him so quickly.

"I've been checking out this marina for a while, looking for a place to keep my boat. I've seen him come and go. The guy wears cowboy boots! Who goes on a boat wearing cowboy boots?"

Charlestraton joined me in a conspiratorial laugh.

"Come to think of it, you're right. Just a social visitor, I guess."

I waved the subject away and engaged him on his boat and the marina and let him talk himself out. Then I shook his hand again and thanked him.

"Your welcome, uh . . ."

Charlestraton scratched the back of his head.

"Vic," I said, with a friendly nod.

Despite his effort to implant the name in his memory, Charlestraton had already forgotten it. They always do.

***

Back at the office, a blinking red light indicated a message on my phone. It was Mark Franklin, asking me to return his call. He'd left his cell number and I got him right away.

"Officer Mark Franklin."

"Let me guess, you've got tickets to a Nats game."

"No, although that can be arranged. I've got the interim report on that death at Daingerfield Island. Want to see it?"

"Sure. You want my email?"

"I was hoping you'd come by and pick it up."

"You really expect me to drop what I'm doing and drive into DC when you can have it in my in-box in five minutes?"

"We could kill two birds with one stone this way. I'm gonna have to talk to you about this sooner or later."

"Give me half an hour."

Franklin met me in a small, dingy waiting room inside the station, where he handed me the form inside an unaddressed and unsealed business envelope. I took it out and scanned it while he watched me.

"It's just preliminary," he said.

"I see that."

Jake had died of drowning secondary to cerebral trauma. Under Cause of Death, the "Accident" box was checked, but so was the one marked "Pending."

"So, the fall did kill him?"

"He wouldn't have drowned if he hadn't hit his head, if that's what you mean."

"You dragged me down here for this?"

"Let's go for a walk."

The cherry blossoms were budding across the way on Hains Point and there was enough of a breeze to ripple the river, but the early spring briskness was gone from the air. The broad promenade was separated from the river by a metal railing and we walked along for a time before either of us spoke. I knew the drill. Mark was waiting for me to open the conversation. When he saw that I wouldn't bite, he pinched the bridge of his nose and launched right in.

"Guy lives on a boat, he gets drunk, he falls, hits his head, and drowns. No witnesses. It's an interim report, but I don't see it changing."

"And?"

"Except that the wife seems to have a boyfriend who happens to be your client."

"He's a friend of the family."

"Business or personal?"

"Does it matter?"

"Not to me. But there *is* something that bothers me. How come Frank Racker thinks he needs a lawyer? Only thing I can come up with is because he's having an affair with the wife."

"You're getting a little close to the attorney-client relationship here, aren't you?"

"I can't put this down till the ends are tied up."

I stopped, pivoted and looked at him as if I'd reached a sudden conclusion.

"You know anything about sovereign immunity?"

"Enough. All claims for injury damage are barred against the sovereign, you know, the government. The government is immune, so you can't bring a claim for injury or wrongful death, based on the government's mistake or negligence."

I nodded.

"Alright, think about what I've been considering. The marina is not supposed to allow liveaboards, but they do; at least they did in one case. They know Carter's a lush, because he gets drunk at the marina bar. They know it's dangerous for a guy like that to be sleeping alone on a boat; anybody with a brain knows that. If your husband drowns in those circumstances, a lot of people will assume they have a wrongful death case against the marina. And they would be right if it was a private marina. But you and I know differently."

His eyes drifted out to the river.

"Because you can't sue the federal government for allowing the circumstances that resulted in Carter's death."

"And the United States government owns the marina."

"And this is the reason you're nosing around?"

We resumed our stroll.

"I'm not going to tell you anything about my conversations with my client."

"But your client is Racker. Unless you're telling me that Carter's wife and Racker really are an item."

We'd come back around the promenade to the station.

"What I'm telling you is, he'd be one of the first ones she'd go to for advice."

"This is gonna keep going around in circles, isn't it?"

"It is, until you realize there's nothing there. Woman's lost her husband. She's trying to figure out what her options are for the rest of her life. So, she talks to her husband's financial adviser. Is that so awful?"

Mark Franklin studied me as he slowly shoved his hands into his pockets.

"Let me think about it."

***

I went home, took a shower and then a nap, the most uninterrupted sleep I'd had in days. When I got up, I felt refreshed for the first time I could remember. I caught Jenny on her cell phone. She sounded frosty and I realized I hadn't called her in a week. I explained that it had not been my intention to ignore her.

"I'm sorry, Jenny."

I fished for an excuse.

"I've been occupied by a pretty stressful case."

"Stressful? Try dancing for a living."

"I'm sure I wouldn't have been the best company. Dinner tonight?"

She hesitated.

"I've got plans."

"All right."

I took a deep breath.

"UVA plays at Maryland on Saturday. Do you want to go?"

"Plays what?"

She sounded impatient.

"Lacrosse."

"Don't know anything about it."

"Well, if you're going to go to school in Charlottesville, it's time you learned."

"Okay."

She gave in and beguiled me with that tinkling laugh.

"I forgot that you're my personal orientation program."

"Maybe we'll have dinner after the game."

I was happy to have a chance to show her I had a social circle.

"A number of my friends will be there, and I want to show you off."

"I don't like being shown off."

I had stepped in it again and the conversation didn't last much longer. I gave her a time and told her I'd pick her up.

I hung up, ruefully aware that my best social intentions always seemed to butt up against my limited store of social graces. I wondered if she felt this too.

Chapter Eighteen

Claim Denied

Track showed up the next day at my office, unannounced. He didn't apologize or ask if I was busy, and my attempt at small talk went nowhere. He was surly and primed for a fight, but rather than take offense, I viewed this as a clue that another shoe had already dropped.

"You know, Track, you've got enough troubles without taking on your lawyer."

He sulked for a bit, then stared at me, his index finger playing with the tip of his nose. Recognizing the signs of indecision, I waited. At last, he impulsively reached into his jacket, pulled out a letter and threw it on my desk.

As soon as I saw what it was, I took my time with it, giving Track time to seethe. It was from an adjuster with a Bailey's Crossroads insurance company, stating that the insurer was withholding coverage under the Carter life insurance policy, pending an investigation into Jake's cause of death. When I looked up, he was fuming.

"What's this bullshit? The policy covers accidental death."

"You want a bottle of water?"

"I want you to answer my question."

"What's your question?"

"Can they get away with this bullshit?"

"So, you already made a claim under the policy?"

"Why not? He's dead."

"Jesus, Track, couldn't you wait for his body to settle into the ground?'

"He was cremated."

Track grabbed the letter back from me and scanned it quickly.

"It says here that loss 'appears to have been caused by an excluded event.' What the hell does that mean?"

"That he died as a result of something that wasn't covered under the policy."

"An accident . . ."

"Yeah, that would be a covered event."

"So . . ."

"So, maybe they think Jake knocked himself on the head, dove under F Dock and committed suicide. Or, maybe they think you and his wife had something to do with it."

He stared at me while he composed himself.

"That's crazy."

"What's crazy is that they sent this letter at all. What's the rush? They don't even have a final death certificate."

I swiveled my chair and watched the crane operating on the construction site across the street. I needed a minute to think this through.

"Are you asking me?"

"You can wait to respond, but I don't think this is going to change."

I reached across and grabbed the letter back.

"The only purpose of this letter is to let you know that sooner or later you'll have to sue them to enforce the policy. Of course, you'll get your attorney's fees if you win."

I added that as maliciously as I could.

"What a bunch of crap."

I stroked my chin.

"It's possible that they're baiting you into suing. Because if you do, then everything's on the table."

"What's 'everything?' "

I shrugged.

"They'll be entitled to ask you about your relationship with Maureen. And they'll ask her about it, too. And they'll ask a lot of questions about the last time you saw Jake. Maybe they don't think you'll take the risk."

"Of course, if I don't sue . . ."

"If you don't sue, people will wonder why."

"You know who's behind this, don't you? Phil Knott."

I thought I'd heard the last of that officious government vulture.

"Phil Knott? What does he care?"

"He's had it in for me all along."

I let that settle, then looked at Track and waited.

"What are my options?"

"Let's wait for the final coroner's report. We ought to have that soon. Then we'll talk about filing suit."

"I'm not sure I want to do that."

"I'm sure. But it might not be as bad as you think."

"Well, they're not paying me."

"I doubt if they've concluded that they're off the hook. It might just be a shot in the dark. They may just be trying to assume a strong negotiating position."

I made a throwaway gesture.

"The whole thing might be a game. But if they sense they've struck a nerve . . ."

"They haven't struck anything, Joth."

With that, Track got up and began pacing my office.

"Another thing. I've also got a client who knows Jake's dead and she's barking at me for her cut of the proceeds of the policy, or that asshole Gray Grayson is, anyway. I need to negotiate a settlement now or this is going to get messy. Can I do that?"

"I think so. That's probably all they really want—to cut their losses."

"If I make a deal, does that reduce what I have to pay the other people?"

"People?"

"There's a lot of money at stake."

"I'm aware. Well, they can certainly withhold payment until the investigation is over. You'd have to offer a pretty big haircut to get them to settle before that. But that would come out of your share."

He winced.

"Am I gonna win if I sue?"

"That's the tricky part. They're not bound by the police investigation. The standard of proof for a crime is 'beyond a reasonable doubt,' but they can deny coverage if it's more likely than not that Jake died as a result of a non-covered event. And if that becomes an issue, they can ask a lot of questions you won't want to answer."

"But if I settle?"

"If you settle, it stays settled."

"I'm not a patient man, Joth. I got a lady who wants her cut."

I stood up. Track's presence was beginning to annoy me.

"If you want me to settle it, I'll see what I can do."

"You get this settled and you'll get your fee."

He left without saying goodbye.

In that day's mail, I got a healthy check from Dan Crowley for my work on the buyout, so I was feeling pretty flush for a change. Ethics are sometimes just a function of practical considerations.

Chapter Nineteen

Orange and Very Blue

Saturday was the first perfect day of spring. As I walked up Jenny's steps, I saw her roommate Gala, seated on a glider on the porch. She turned her pale face my way. "You seen my cat?"

"I didn't know you had a cat."

"Oh yeah, I got a cat. He's a tabby."

Her eyes were distracted, and I looked at her carefully.

"That's nice."

"He kills mice. His name is Mellow Yellow."

I nodded.

"I'll let you know if I see him."

I was about to knock, but Jenny opened the door like she'd been waiting for me. I was distracted by Gala and said the first thing that came into my head.

"You look great."

It was true. She wore a green sundress that fit her as if it had been custom designed. Jenny looked great in clothes, and I wondered, not for the first time, if this would be the day I finally saw her without them.

"I thought you'd wear orange and blue."

The thought seemed to surprise her as she took in my navy polo with the school logo on the breast.

"Should I change?"

"Do you have anything in the school colors?"

"I don't think so. Something light blue, maybe."

I looked at my watch.

"No, you'll be all right. At least you're not wearing red."

As we stepped off the porch, I turned to speak to Gala, but something in Jenny's manner froze me. Each of the two roommates acted as if the other didn't exist. Down on the sidewalk, I held open the passenger door and as Jenny got in, I asked what had been burning in my head all along.

"Everything okay with you two?"

"Oh yeah, fine," she said through a weary sigh. "She's not a bad person, but I will be glad to be rid of her."

"I hope she finds her cat."

"Gala doesn't have a cat. Get it?"

I considered myself to be a person of above average insight, but when personal stakes clouded the issue, I could be as obtuse as an adolescent.

"You mean she never had one?"

"She has an imaginary cat."

"I see."

About a mile into the drive, I picked up on that comment and remembered what Chris had said about Gala.

"You know, you could move out now, Jenny, if you'd like."

"No, the dorms don't open 'til August."

"You could move in with me. You know, just for the summer."

I snuck a glance at her. Her brow was furrowed, and I could see she was searching for a tactful response.

"Well, never mind. A little premature."

"I haven't heard from you in a week, Joth, and suddenly you think I'm going to move in with you?"

"You're right."

I winced.

"I've had a pretty big case. It's been troubling. Sorry."

She raised a hand dismissively.

"I'm sorry. I've had a rough week, too."

"Has this got to do with Gala?"

"Yes. She needs some help."

"Are you going to try to get her some?"

"It's Saturday morning. It's a beautiful day. Let's start over."

I smiled.

"I like your car."

I drove a functional and non-descript Volvo with a lot of hard miles on it.

"It's not a BMW."

As she looked at me, I could see the gears turning.

"I did tell you that once, didn't I, that lawyers drive BMWs? Can't believe you remembered."

"I remember a lot of things. It's a professional necessity."

"I forget a lot of things for the same reason."

We crossed over the Potomac on the Wilson Bridge and followed the Beltway around to College Park. Both schools had top-level lacrosse programs and the intense Virginia-Maryland rivalry had a long history.

I parked under a tree at the edge of the south lot and joined hundreds of couples and small groups, dressed in orange and blue and red and white, all moving toward the separate gatherings of their tribes.

A number of UVA groups had set up orange and blue-striped pavilion tents along a strip of asphalt at the back of the lot. One of these bore a sign in oversized letters, welcoming UVA lacrosse alumni. A substantial crowd had already gathered. In the back of the tent, the oldest of the old boys and their wives were playing beach music, enjoying drinking games, and dancing the shag, just as they had in their twenties.

I put a cooler of drinks on a table and started scanning the group, nodding at familiar faces of old teammates and younger acquaintances I'd made over the years at these events. Someone called my name: Dash Brehm, a midfielder I'd played with for three years in what seemed a distant lifetime. I recognized his still-adorable wife, but he was slapping my shoulder before I could come up with her name.

"Joth Proctor! When's the last time we saw you at one of these things?"

I cast a glance at a knot of grizzled old boys at the back of the tents.

"Can't live in the past, Dash."

"It'd be shame to forget it. Have a drink, Joth, you old dog."

He handed me a red Solo cup before I could ask what was in it."

"This is my friend, Jenny."

She smiled and accepted the cup.

Dash was already drunk, and he probably would have felt as awkward as an underdressed wedding guest, if he hadn't been.

"You remember Donna?" he said, introducing his wife.

"Of course, how are you, Donna?"

Donna was a trooper. Even as an undergrad, she'd been the tactful and gracious buffer who kept her husband out of the social hot water.

"Did I hear your name as Jenny?"

She asked smoothly, with the smile of a professional hostess.

"Yes."

Donna wore her hair in the same shoulder-length cut she'd worn in college, and quite possibly was wearing the very same orange and blue sundress she'd worn to her husband's last game.

"Well Joth, you certainly seem to be spending your time in improved company."

Everyone laughed except Jenny.

"Jenny's heading to the nursing school this fall."

Dash and Donna expressed sincere congratulations at her inclusion in the group and Jenny's eyes sparkled as she warmed to them.

"I can see I'm going to have to get myself some clothes."

This evidence of wit was a more reliable passkey than her coming matriculation. The gang took the opportunity to poke fun at my long-standing reputation for sartorial inelegance and we were soon joined by several other couples anxious to participate in our rite of mutual abuse.

Jenny finished her drink and handed me her cup while chuckling at somebody else's effort to rib an old teammate. We were drinking bourbon in the afternoon, and I was glad to get her another one.

I was hoping Track wouldn't show up, but he did. He had twice been an All-American and was accorded the deference which that status commanded. He was not the sort of guy whose absence would be regretted, but he was there, a big man among big men, set up in a corner of the tent—alone, drinking steadily and eyeing the group like a petty potentate, marking potential challengers to his throne.

Dash was as dismayed as I was. It was his shoulder that Track had broken with the cheap shot in the alumni game many years ago. As Dash eyed him, he winced and instinctively rotated the damaged joint.

"Still hurt?" I said.

"Nah. Not much. Only when it's cold, really."

"He ever apologize to you?"

"Apologize. That son of bitch never apologized to anybody for anything."

"Hello, Jade."

Track's commanding voice silenced the laughter and the group turned toward him.

"Jenny," she said, with obvious trepidation.

"Do you two know each other?"

257

Donna asked with a clumsy sincerity.

"Yeah, I know her," said Track. "Her name's Jade."

Donna could smell a social crisis from a mile off.

"It's because of her eyes, Dash. I guess you shouldn't have worn that green dress, Jenny."

She took her arm.

"Of course, if I had eyes like that, I'd wear green, too. Come on, Jenny, let's go get a drink."

She took Jenny's arm and led her away.

I tended not to see the simmering malice in Track that others did. I didn't believe he meant any harm; he was simply a blunt instrument, as unconscious of the power of his words as he was aware of the pain he was capable of delivering with a fearsome body check.

Dash took a look at him and turned his attention to me.

"Maybe we ought to get to our seats, huh? Let's pick up the girls."

It was still fifteen minutes before gametime, but I agreed.

***

It was a crisply played, physical game. By the time the offenses opened up in the second half, I'd explained the rudiments of the game to Jenny: the arcane off-sides and possession rules, and enough about offensive strategy for her to enjoy the competition. By the end, she was lightly sunburned and slightly intoxicated like the rest of us and seemed invested in the ups and downs of her school.

Traffic was heavy leaving the stadium and it was a long drive back. Perhaps the bourbon and sun had worn Jenny down. My efforts at conversation drew terse responses and she shifted her posture in the seat as if she was in a hurry to get home. Back at her place, we sat on the glider on the porch, where I put my arm around her slim, warm shoulder. Neither the sun nor the alcohol had been excessive by themselves. Jenny had a glow to her skin, but her mood was dour and reserved. I leaned forward to kiss her, but when I persisted, she pushed me away.

"That offer to move in. That was serious."

She paused to gather her thoughts.

"I'm not sure that's the best idea."

I studied the ceiling fan above the glider, watching its unmoving blades.

"What's that mean?"

"It means things are going a little fast in my life right now."

"It's a lot of change."

I thought again of Gala and her imaginary cat.

"But isn't that good?"

"I need some space, Joth. I'm starting a new life where nobody knows me, and nobody knows me as Jade."

"No one's going to know you as Jade."

"Some of your friends do."

"Track is not my friend."

"He's your client. He's part of your group,"

"None of those guys can stand him. Neither can I, to tell you the truth."

She discounted this.

"And if I'm with you, here or in Charlottesville, I'll still be Jade to them."

I failed to find a response.

"It doesn't mean I don't want to see you, Joth. Let's just step back for a while."

"For how long?"

She recalculated.

"I don't want to be Jade. I don't want anybody to know me as Jade."

I was as glad to put Jade in the past as she was, but I had no magic wand to make it disappear.

"You're Jenny to me. Will you think about it?"

"You are sweet. I'll think about it."

"You want me to come in?"

"Not tonight."

"But you'll think about it?"
"Yes, I'll think about it."

Chapter Twenty

Fink's Game

The insurance adjuster's name was Bob Fink. I called the number on the letterhead and got a perky and youthful sounding voice. I identified myself and asked to speak to Mr. Fink.

"May I ask what this is about?"

"A claim on a policy on the life of Jacob Carter."

I read the claim number off the letter.

"I represent the beneficiary."

"Let me see if Mr. Fink is in."

She was back on in a moment to announce that he was not.

"I see. Can I make an appointment to see him?"

She hesitated.

"He's on vacation."

I counted to five.

"You'll get better at blowing people off as you get older. I want to talk to him. Now."

"Hold please."

I got to listen to almost an entire Barry Manilow song as I waited. Then, I heard a crisp voice.

"This is Robert Fink."

"Hello Mr. Fink, how was your vacation?"

"This is likely to be a short conversation."

"But that won't make the problem go away."

"What problem?"

"Your problem, Mr. Fink. Your bad faith denial of coverage."

He was waiting for that one and laughed.

"You can file suit, counselor, that's your remedy. But you already know that. Of course, you might not want certain things to get out."

"Since when is an insurance adjuster an enforcer of Virginia public policy?"

"Good day, counselor."

If Fink had caught me on a better day, or if he hadn't gone out of his way to piss me off, that might have been the end of it. But it wasn't. So, I went out for a beer and then another and thought it through again.

A lawsuit claiming a bad faith denial of claim was a realistic response and a serious threat. To deny the claim before receiving the final coroner's report is an invitation to be sued. An experienced adjuster would recognize that likelihood and take steps to avoid it.

This meant that Fink knew things that put Track at sufficient risk to make a lawsuit imprudent. And what would those things be? It had to be more than Track's possible involvement in Carter's death. If that was it, Fink would simply wait for the final report before denying the claim. Besides, he was an insurance adjuster and used to the malice inherent in the human heart.

No, that wouldn't generate the sort of vindictiveness I heard in Fink's voice. No matter how I looked at it, it came back to Knott. Somebody was blackmailing Knott, and whether or not Track was behind it didn't matter, because Knott probably thought he was.

Back at the office, a quick Internet search turned up immediate gold. Both Knott and Fink had graduated from the Virginia Military Institute, where they were one class apart. A much smaller school than UVA, VMI was renowned for the strength and depth of the bonds between alumni.

It was half past one. I pulled up Knott's phone number and placed the call, gambling that he'd be at lunch. He was. I emitted a frustrated sound to his receptionist.

"He and I have an appointment for lunch later this week. I'm sorry, my computer crashed."

I gave him a dramatic sigh.

"We're lunching at the Shirlington Grand."

A bored male voice responded.

"He has an appointment for tomorrow with Mr. Easterly."

"That's me."

I remembered Knott commenting on his preferred lunch hour.

"At one o'clock, right?"

"That's correct."

"By the way, that's 'Eastly.' Someone must have written it down wrong."

He tapped a pencil.

"Walter Easterly, Merrifield Auto Parts?"

"Eastly," I repeated. "Close enough. All right, I'll see him there."

I thanked him and hung up. Then I called Walter Easterly at Merrifield Auto Parts and cancelled his lunch date with Phil Knott.

***

The next day, I arrived at the bar at the Shirlington Grand a little before one. The slender girl with the dirty blonde hair was behind the bar.

"Hi Darla."

I slid onto a stool.

I had poked pretty deeply into my closet for the linen pants, pink shirt and blue blazer I was wearing. She studied me for a quick moment and decided I was harmless, just another aging single guy who thought he knew her.

"Hi," she said, sounding cautious.

I bounced off the stool and extended my hand.

"Dan. Dan McGrew. Medical sales? Well, it was pretty busy last time I came in."

"Oh, now I remember," she said cheerfully. "Get you something?"

"Tequila Sunrise?"

"Coming right up."

The bar was quiet. A single guy at the other end tried to make eye contact with me in the mirror, but I froze him with a nasty scowl.

"Here you are."

Darla smiled as she put the drink down. I lifted it before she could turn away.

"Here's to you."

I took a loud sip.

"Had a good day today."

"Did you?"

I shook my head, amazed at my own success.

"This digital imaging equipment! It's changing all the time and every doctor has to have it. Guaranteed malpractice if they don't. It's like selling bread to a starving man."

"Really?"

"Really. A girl like you, so young and pretty . . . I don't know what you're doing, working here."

For a moment, Darla's eyes drifted.

"Looking for the right opportunity, I guess."

"Everybody's doing that. The secret is knowing where to look."

She took a long moment to size me up, and as she did, I caught a glimpse of Phil Knott as he entered through the revolving door. He threw a wave at Darla and took the stairs two at a time.

"There's Phil!" I said.

She glanced up and her eyes registered recognition and surprise. She giggled. "Phil Knott?"

"You know him?"

She backtracked.

"No, not really. Not any better than you. He comes in here from time to time."

I glanced at my watch.

"Well, he's a son of a bitch. Late as usual."

I paid for my drink and went upstairs.

Having not spotted his lunch date, Knott was at the top of the stairs, about to start back down. I put four fingers and a thumb on his chest and pushed him back firmly.

"Hi, Phil. Lunch?"

His face clouded as he tried to place me.

"I've got plans for lunch."

"Yeah, with Walter Easterly. That's me. At least it is today. Shall we sit down?"

I led him to a table. By the time we sat down, he had recalled my face and figured out who I was.

"If you like fish," I said, "try the trout."

Knott fiddled with a cuff link.

"What's this all about?"

"Bob Fink. College buddy of yours, isn't he?"

"I knew him in college, so what?"

"How well do you know him now?"

As his brow furrowed, I could sense Knott's indignation.

"What is this, a shakedown?"

"Shakedown?"

I laughed.

"I just want some answers."

"What kind of answers?"

"Your buddy, Fink, denied coverage under the viatical that Frank Racker owned on Jake Carter's life."

Knott's face reddened.

"What's that got to do with me?"

"The body's barely cold."

"That's between them, not me."

"Fink's your buddy. You put him up to it."

"That's ridiculous."

Knott's tone was insistent, but he squirmed in his chair.

"Why would I do that? We're friends, yes, but I hardly ever see him."

I leaned forward and summoned an amiable tone.

"Phil, whoever was blackmailing you, it wasn't Halftrack Racker."

He paused and wet his lips.

"I don't know what you're talking about,"

His reply was so predictably somber that it gave him away.

"Sure, you do, Phil. But so far, you and I are the only ones who do. And it can stay that way."

"How do you know it's not Racker?"

"Because blackmail's not his style, for one thing."

"But it's yours?"

"No, but I'll find out who it is. And I'll make 'em stop."

Knott stared at his plate.

"If what?"

"If you talk to Fink. Just tell him to do his job."

"His job?"

"His job is a good faith negotiation with me on the Carter policy. That's all I want."

"And you'll take care of the other thing?"

"I'll do what I can."

"Not much of a guarantee."

"You're in the insurance business, Phil. It's a good bet, statistically. Now, what do you know that could help me?"

Knott tilted his head as he thought something through.

"Mr. Proctor, it was a woman's voice that called."

"What did she say?"

"She said she knows about what goes on here sometimes. That other people might have to know about it, you know."

"Did she mention Racker by name?"

He nodded.

"She said he didn't know she was calling, that she thought what the bureau was doing on the policy was unfair to him."

"Did she make a particular demand?"

"No."

He shook his head.

"I think she thought I got the message."

"Did you check with your receptionist desk? The caller's number would have come up on the phone."

"No, no, I didn't. I know I should have but uh, I was pretty shaken up."

"I understand."

"Do you know who the caller was?"

I told him no, but I realized it was a woman with an interest in the viatical. It couldn't have been Alice Moriarty. It was someone with an imaginary cat.

"And Bobby?" he said.

He gave an expansive wave of his hand.

"He's got nothing to do with what goes on here."

"Bobby?"

"Mr. Fink."

"Ah yes, your good friend, Bobby. If he does what I ask, he'll be forgotten as soon as the file on the claim closes. Do we understand each other?"

Knott folded his hands and dropped his eyes.

"Yes."

"Thanks for buying lunch."

On the way out, I stopped downstairs at the hostess stand and asked for a business envelope. After a bit of searching, the maître de found one. I thanked him and walked to the bar, where I jotted a brief note on the back of my business card, asking the recipient to call me. I put it in the envelope and sealed it. Then, I waited for Darla to make her way over.

"Are you familiar with Bob Fink?"

You could see the antennae pop up as she picked up my change in demeanor.

"I'm not sure."

"You know him, Darla. Can you make sure he gets this?"

"I can try. Can't make any promises."

I jotted the name on the envelope.

"He'll be expecting it."

I left ten dollars on the bar.

Chapter Twenty-One

Mama's Ice Cream

On the way back to the office, I swung by Taunton Acres to see if Dan had taken Mama for her drive and her ice cream. She was in the same place I'd found her on my last visit, seated in front of the gas fireplace in the parlor, but instead of staring glumly into the glowing logs, she was flipping through a book of historic photographs of Arlington County.

When I touched her shoulder, she turned her head a few degrees, and then her eyes rotated just enough to meet mine. As she smiled, I saw a light of recognition in her eyes.

"You feeling okay, Mama?"

She nodded.

I asked about her health and her friends and her memory seemed sharp.

"I understand Dan came by."

"Yes, he did."

"What did you do?"

"We went for a drive."

"Dan took you for a drive?"

"Yes, yes he did. And he took me for ice cream," she said, with adolescent enthusiasm.

I smiled and patted her shoulder and we talked of long-ago things for what seemed only a few minutes, but when I looked at my watch, a full half an hour had passed. As I pushed up to my feet and looked down on Mama's frail form, I wondered if I'd ever see her again or if she'd ever enjoy another drive and ice cream.

It wasn't that I doubted Dan Crowley; I just wanted to confirm the story before I left. As I stopped by the reception desk, I was surprised to see the somewhat familiar face of Melanie Freeman. She must have come on duty while I was visiting with Mama.

"Well, Mr. Proctor!" she said cheerfully. "Most of our visitors come to see friends or relatives. For you, maybe it's clients?"

"Maybe. So, I see you've gotten started here."

Melanie was wearing a lavender dress imprinted with spring flowers in pastel hues, which seemed to add brightness to her eyes and cheeks.

"Yes, thanks to you and your friend, Master Tran."

"Master Tran?"

I chuckled.

"You mean DP?"

"Yes, I do. I don't even think I know him, but he was good enough to put in a word for me."

I smiled and shook my head. DP had an undeniable glibness when he put his mind to a task.

"How's it working out so far?"

"It's all pretty new, but I like the people."

"Do you mind if I take a look through the sign-in sheets?"

I gestured toward the clipboard.

She frowned.

"Well, I don't know. That seems rather irregular."

I realized I was putting her on the spot, but the awkward moment passed when Norma Tompkins emerged from the office behind the desk.

"You just can't stay away, can you?"

I laughed and raised my hands as if I'd been caught, then explained the purpose of my inquiry.

"Dan Crowley promised me he'd take Mrs. Barkley for a drive. I'm just following up to make sure he did."

"Yes, indeed. I hear they went for quite a drive. They even stopped for ice cream. This had a marvelous effect on Christine."

I filled my lungs with a sense of a job well done, and Norma picked up on my reaction.

"Shall I assume you're behind this?"

"No, just facilitating it."

"I'll bet he was," Melanie said, chirping right up to vouch for me.

"He fixes things, you know."

Norma smiled, nodded and returned to her office. As I smiled at Melanie, her phone message from the previous week bubbled back into my head.

"And at a bargain rate, too, huh?"

"That's right!" she said.

***

On the way back, I called Riding Time and asked if Jade was working. I knew that the person I was looking for wouldn't be there if she was. That person was Chris Barkley, and he was tucking a ten-dollar bill in someone's G-string when I walked in. I waited until he was finished, an act he executed with a panache born of long experience, and then I tapped him on the shoulder.

"Hey, Mr. Joth. Here to see Jade?"

"No, I'm here to see you."

I gestured over my shoulder to an empty booth and he followed me.

"Are you working?"

"Yeah. I got a job at the Braddock Road Garden Center. Botany, you know? I always liked plants, and there are nice people there."

"What are you going to be doing there?"

"Learning the business, I hope. Start from the bottom up, like Dan did with Mama. There's a lot of things to learn there."

I nodded, hoping he'd learn more about the gardening business than he had digested about running a gentlemen's club. The table had not been wiped after the last patrons. I pulled a napkin from the dispenser and mopped up the dregs of drying beer.

"Well, Chris, I hope you're behaving yourself."

"Is that why you're here?" he said in a peevish voice. "Checking up on me?"

"Nope. Got something for you to sign."

I motioned for the waitress.

"Is Dan around? Tell him I need to see him. And tell him to bring his checkbook."

While we waited, I had another thing I wanted to ask him about.

"You know a guy named Phil Knott?"

His face reddened.

"I don't think I do."

"I'm glad I don't have to put you on the stand, because you're a terrible liar."

He opened his hands and glanced around, as if looking for someone else to answer the question.

"I've never talked to him myself."

I nodded.

"Okay, then. Who did?"

He craned his neck for a waitress and ordered a beer. I shook her off when she asked what I wanted. Chris got belligerent as soon as the waitress left.

"Talked to him about what?"

"I learned some compromising information about Mr. Knott. It came out of this bar. You knew about it, but you weren't the only one. Who else knew?"

"Could have been anybody. It's hard to keep a secret around here."

"The person I'm looking for owed Track Racker."

I could see the wheels turning as soon as I mentioned Track's name. I guessed he wasn't debating the answer but whether he should tell me.

"Somebody who owed him money?"

"That's right, Chris."

"There's a girl over at the sports pub. She's always behind with him."

"What's her name?"

"Gala," he said.

He said it grudgingly. It didn't surprise me, and I tried not to show it.

"Gala? Jade's roommate?"

Chris looked at me, said nothing and bit his lower lip.

"She owed him money?"

"I don't know, Mr. Proctor. Something like that. Money from a business deal."

"What kind of business deal?"

He dropped his eyes.

"I don't know much about it. Just what I heard."

I pushed back from the table and folded my arms, but before I could speak a jovial Dan Crowley joined us.

"Today's the day we close this thing?" he said, as he slid in beside Chris.

I opened my briefcase on the table.

"That's the plan."

It was all there: stock certificates, the promissory note, two original copies of the settlement agreement and the various attachments.

"You got your checkbook, Dan?'

"Already wrote it out."

It didn't take long. I explained the documents and the details, but neither one of them was listening. Dan wanted it done and Chris was focused on the check, like it represented the first real meal he'd had in a week.

As soon as we signed, Dan shook our extended hands, and as he moved to depart, I held his for an extra moment.

"She appreciated it, Dan."

He winked at me.

"It was the right thing to do."

I watched him head back toward his office. Then, I asked Chris if he still intended to head for the islands.

"I don't know, Mr. Proctor. This is a lot of money."

"You might need a financial planner, but don't hire one without talking to me."

He nodded, but I knew I'd never hear from him again. God help him if Track got hold of him, but he was a big boy.

"About Gala," I said, but Chris was already getting up.

"I've gotta go. Jade will be here soon, and you know the deal. Can't be around."

He was right, of course. I didn't say anything, and Chris disappeared. When the waitress came by, I ordered a beer and sipped it as I thought through the various Riding Time connections. I had another after that and perhaps a third. When I looked at my watch, I was surprised how late it had gotten. I paid the tab and left.

Outside, in the brighter light of Crystal City, the rush hour traffic was gathering, with its typical mix of honks and shouts. The air was thick with the odor of exhaust, held down overhead by masses of descending storm clouds. As I turned up 23rd Street, I came face to face with Jenny, arriving for her shift. She stopped short and put her hand to her chest.

"Jesus, you scared me."

Startled, I backed away a step.

"Jade . . . Jenny . . . I'm surprised. What are you doing here?"

She flashed a look of annoyance and stepped around me like a starlet avoiding paparazzi.

"I'm late," she said. "I'll give you a call."

I turned and began to speak, but an image flashed through my mind of Chris Barkley getting kicked in the nuts. As I watched Jenny walk away, I understood that our relationship was sliding away and that I'd fumbled another chance to retrieve it. I drove home, wondering how many more chances I'd get.

Chapter Twenty-Two

The Price of Temptation

The call from Bob Fink came two days later. In the interim, the final coroner's report came down, and that helped.

Fink acted like we'd never spoken, which was as good a way as any to reboot things.

"I'm calling about the Carter life insurance policy. I believe you represent the claimant?"

"Yes, I do, Mr. Fink. I wanted to talk to you about the denial of the claim."

I wish all negotiations went as smoothly as that one. There was no posturing and no dissembling, which is not to say it was an easy negotiation, but the entire discussion remained grounded in fact and law. He was tenacious, made valid points, and gave ground grudgingly. In the end, the coroner's conclusion of accidental drowning was hard to get around.

"I'm authorized to pay you eighty percent of the policy value, Mr. Proctor. That's the best I can do."

"Let me talk to my client."

***

I was weary of talking to clients. Track, Jade, Chris, even Dan: they all posed complications or seemed to have ulterior motives. The only recent exception had been Melanie Freeman, who'd been everything you could want in a criminal client: honest, repentant and grateful. I remembered again her glowing words.

"You're worth every bit of 300 dollars an hour."

Then, the implication of what she'd said finally filtered through my thick head. Three hundred dollars an hour? But I was only charging Father John $250 an hour and the church was picking up some portion of that reduced amount. I picked up the phone and called Taunton Acres, hoping I could catch Melanie there. She was still at the reception desk and answered the phone.

"Did you call to take me up on the dinner offer?"

There was a perky cheerfulness in her voice, a self-effacing friendliness that would have made another excuse difficult, but I moved past it.

"Three hundred dollars an hour," I said.

"What about it?"

"You said I charge $300 an hour."

"Don't you?"

"Yes, and I'm worth it, too. But how did you know?"

"That's what Father John said you charge."

"But not in your case."

"I don't understand."

"I charged you a reduced fee. Father John said he'd collect part of my fee from you and make up the difference from a church fund. That's why he wanted me to send the bills to the church. What did you pay?"

"$300. He said it was a reduced amount."

"I charged Father John $250."

"What does this mean?"

"It means Father John is raking fifty dollars an hour off what you paid him and giving me what's left."

"There must be some mistake."

"Oh, there's a mistake all right."

"It can't be."

"Are you sure of your numbers?"

"Of course."

She sounded bewildered.

"What should I do?"

"Nothing, leave it to me."

"What are you going to do?"

"I'm gonna go home and take a cold shower."

***

If I'd had any brains, that's what I would have done. I would have gone home, taken a cold shower, and calmly confronted Father John in the morning, but if I had any brains, I wouldn't have been defending petty crimes at discount rates.

I was rarely offended by crimes or criminals. People are human; they succumb to want, temptation and anger, and my job was to help them recover from their bad choices, not to judge them. But occasionally I ran into an act so cynical and unjust that I couldn't and wouldn't stand for it. What Father John had done touched a nerve I hadn't tamed and didn't want to. I got in my car and drove to St. Carolyn's and parked in a handicapped spot in the chain link-fenced lot.

The afternoon was bright and clear. I was enraged, but my anger hadn't taken control of my wits.

"Where's Father John?"

I demanded of the nun working a Harry Potter-themed jigsaw puzzle on the card table in the parish office. She was young and petite, but she'd been around long enough to know how to deal with irate males.

"He's not here right now."

She calmly rose to her feet.

"Where is he?"

Her eyebrows shot up in alarm and she peeked briefly over her shoulder at a hedge-lined garden, visible through the glass door. I headed in that direction. She moved to intercept me but wasn't quick enough.

"You can't go out there!"

I dodged her and went through the door.

The lush, tidy parish grounds were enclosed by the walls of a small campus of buildings, a grotto in the center of busy Arlington. Hedges, shrubs and small fruit trees fringed paths of crushed stone and separated the grounds into a series of intimate gardens, built around iron benches and iconography.

I quickly came upon Father John, contemplating St. Francis feeding the birds. He sized me up immediately and his unruffled and unwelcoming expression showed that he had deduced the purpose of my visit.

"What can I do for you, Mr. Proctor?"

"Two fifty an hour."

He nodded calmly, turned and began strolling down the path.

"There are many tranquil places in Arlington. The National Cemetery is one of my favorites, but I prefer the simplicity of this place. In a complex world, it's always calming to be here,"

"You've got some explaining to do."

"We've all got some explaining to do," he said. "Do you recall how Jesus taught his disciples to pray? He instructed them to ask to be delivered from temptation. Temptation. Jesus knew this is the universal pitfall."

"You aren't praying hard enough."

"This is the best place I know to contemplate our frailty."

"You bastard. What are you going to tell Melanie Freeman to pray for?"

"Melanie Freeman will understand. There are many less fortunate than her and we all need to do what we can."

His persistent calm when confronted with his hypocrisy infuriated me.

"And you are certainly one of them, you son of a bitch."

"If you're going to talk like that, I'm going to have to ask you to leave."

He shouldn't have had to ask. I should have understood that this was a matter for Heather now. But some things couldn't be left to the slow and uncertain process of the law. I took a long step forward and punched him hard enough that he fell into an iron bench that occupied a cut out in the hedge. He straightened himself up into a sitting position.

"That was a mistake."

"There's no mistake."

Before I could speak or act, I heard a rustling in the brush beside the path. I turned and caught a glimpse of Jenny, just before she stepped forward and slapped me across the face. I straightened up as if sobered.

"Toiling in the vineyards of the Lord?"

I asked that with all the irony I could muster.

"Get out of here, Joth."

"Your brother's a crook."

"And I told you to leave."

I glanced at Father John, who rubbed his jaw.

"You've got your claws into her, too, don't you?"

I turned on my heel and left.

***

I was still feeling sulky the following afternoon when Track came in. Eighty percent of the proceeds of the policy on Jake Carter's life was a lot of money; at least it was to me. Track didn't think so.

"Christ, I mean, is that the best you could do?" he complained, as he slouched into the client chair in my office.

"We've got options."

"What options?"

"File suit. Of course, that'll take a year, but you'll be entitled to interest on the final judgment."

I made my point in the most offensive tone I could muster.

"You'll have to testify. And there'll be some hungry defense lawyer there, just dying to cross-examine you."

"I'm ready for that."

"Are you? You told me you were at Carter's house the night he died."

"That's right."

"But you also told me you were there the next morning before the police came."

"So?"

"So how did Maureen know her husband was dead?"

Track shifted his eyes away from mine.

"I went back in the morning to check on him. See if he'd come home."

"I assume your phone was dead."

He glowered but didn't answer.

"You told me Jake hit his head."

"He did."

"How did you know that? The police didn't tell you. They just said he drowned."

It took Track a moment to process what I was telling him, but I was ready to wait all day.

"He was drunk," Track said.

His eyes wandered the room then refocused on me.

"Almost seven in the morning and he was still drunk. He fell, hit his head, and went straight into the water."

"You argued?"

Track adjusted his collar.

"Yes."

"About what?"

"Maureen."

"I thought he didn't care about his wife."

"He didn't love her if that's what you mean. It's a matter of possession. Nobody wants another man to take what's his."

"You pushed him?"

"No."

He denied it with an immediacy that suggested a lie.

"He came after me."

"You're half his age and twice his size."

"He picked up a winch handle and came at me. He was drunk, Joth. He lunged and I sidestepped and that was it. He hit his head and I panicked."

"You panicked? That's one thing I've never known you to do."

"I was having an affair with his wife."

"And you had an insurance policy on his life."

He leaned forward and rested his heavy forearms against my desk. His face tightened and his voice became hoarse with emotion.

"I didn't kill him Joth. Not Jake, not a good guy like him. He fell and hit his head."

"You just didn't do anything to try to save him."

"Is that a crime?"

"It'll sure as hell keep you from collecting on that insurance policy."

Track chewed a knuckle and stared at me.

"Makes it pretty easy then, doesn't it?"

"Easy for me. I don't need to live with it."

"Fuck you, Joth."

He started to get up.

"Not so fast, Track. I want to know about Gala."

"I don't know anybody named Gala."

"Jenny's roommate."

"Not anymore," he said, with a snide chuckle.

"Who told you that?"

He looked at me shrewdly.

"I don't miss much."

"More than you think."

Track studied my face for a long moment, his lips pursed thoughtfully.

"Jumping into that pretty fast, aren't you Joth?"

He had me off balance, but he didn't know why. If he thought Jenny and I were moving in together, I wasn't going to disabuse him of that notion. I'd deny him that victory. I changed the subject.

"This deal, this settlement. It's contingent on one more thing. No more calls to or about Phil Knott."

He caught my full meaning from my expression and turned up his hands.

"Who's Phillip Knott?"

"Just make sure it stays that way. And you make sure Gala knows that, too."

***

I made a call to Fink and told him we had a deal. It was an agreeable conversation, the first one I'd had in a while.

"Make the settlement check payable to your trust account?"

"Absolutely."

I spent most of the afternoon drafting the settlement agreement. I emailed it to Track for his approval, and he called an hour later.

"Everything okay?"

"Well, there's one thing."

"What's that?"

"Joth, I got your bill. I need you to take a little less."

"A little less?"

I fumed.

"A little less than what?"

"I'm taking a hit on this, Joth. I think you ought to share it. You know, proportionally."

"You want me to accept eighty percent of my bill in full payment?"

"That's right."

"You haven't even got my final bill yet."

"How much is that?"

"I don't know."

I pulled up his account on my PC and did a little math.

"It'll be a few hundred more. I'm not done with the case yet."

"Joth, you work for yourself. You can charge what you want. It's all profit to you. Can't you write off the last bit?"

"The hell I will."

"I'll tell you what. You take the amount of your current bill out of the settlement check and we'll call it square."

Cash was king with me. I had quoted him a high rate and I had billed every minute I worked on it. There was also real value in being done with him.

I agreed and hung up. It was a steep cut, but it would be worth it to get rid of him.

Chapter Twenty-Three

Joth's Bonus

When Track came in a few days later to sign the agreement, he was grinning broadly, like someone who had just been released from a petty punishment. He tossed a heavy mailing envelope onto my desk and it slid across into my lap. Taped to it was the second fob to the security gate.

"What's this?"

"All yours. For reducing your bill."

I opened the envelope. Inside was the title of the *Southern Patriot*, signed over to me, plus keys to the engine and cabin hatch.

"Everything else, the paperwork and stuff; it's all on board."

"The boat isn't yours to give."

"But it is," he said.

He slid comfortably into one of my client chairs.

I looked at the title, saw Jacob Carter's name above mine, and Maureen Carter's endorsement of the title to me.

"She doesn't want it, and I know you've got some sailing background."

I put a knuckle to my nose and pondered the consequences of such a gift.

"You and Maureen must be getting pretty close."

"I'm her financial advisor, don't forget."

Track winked.

"A boat's just a hole in the water you keep throwing money into," he said, quoting an adage he probably got off a coffee mug. "At least it would be for her. I know you'll make good use of it."

"I don't know if I can accept this."

"Why not?"

He threw up his hands and laughed boisterously.

"Don't be silly. Take me out on it some time. I always wanted Jake to take me for a sail. He never did. You name the time and place and I'll be there. We'll have some laughs and talk things through. In the meantime, I'll see if I can't drum up some more business for you."

It still didn't sit right with me.

"I appreciate it."

That was all I could muster.

Track caught my reluctance.

"Look, Joth, you got me off the griddle. I won't forget that."

It took barely fifteen minutes to explain the terms of the insurance settlement, but Track paid little attention to the details. He signed the paperwork with an elegant flourish, and I told him I'd run the settlement check through my trust account and have his payment to him as soon as it cleared. He got up and embraced me in a fraternal hug.

It was all so easy for him.

Chapter Twenty-Four

Dark News

I had *The Washington Post* delivered daily to my office and the next morning I read through it with my feet on my desk, nursing the only good cup of coffee I'd have all day.

In the Local Digest in the Metro section a short news brief caught my attention: "Woman Found Dead in Del Ray."

It provided the victim's age and a few sketchy details.

"Suspicious circumstances," said the police spokesman. "Investigation continues."

Another day; another suspicious death.

When I finished the Sports section, I spent a few minutes reviewing the inventory Track had delivered of personal items that would come with Jake's boat: five coils of nylon line, four life vests, three dock fenders, two air horns, an extra jib. There was a ship-to-shore radio, a spare anchor and heavy cable, a wooden paddle, a winch handle, Jake's sleeping bag and personal items, a collection of inexpensive pipes and three containers of aromatic tobacco. The list included a variety of hand tools and spare parts, a plastic toolkit with basic tools, a first aid kit, several back issues of *The Civil War Times*, and a replica Civil War cavalry pistol, fully loaded and reported by Track to be in good working order. The inclusion of these items had the effect of personalizing the gift of the boat, a reminder that the owner had been a man that I liked; a man who deserved better than a friend like Track.

I folded my hands behind my head and imagined summer evenings cruising up the Potomac to Hains Point and Nats Park, or south to Mt. Vernon and beyond. Many of my childhood friends raced on summer weekends, but I always saw sailing as a recreation—an escape from the grind of school or sports. Putting my doubts aside, the more I thought about it, the more appropriate Track's gift seemed. Perhaps he wasn't such a son of a bitch after all.

I was still lost in this pleasant reverie when the phone rang.

It was Heather. She sounded tense and without any preliminaries she invited herself over.

"Something going on?'

"Yes," she said. "Something's going on."

I was sure I knew what this was about: Father John had lodged a complaint against me. I expected her to deliver an assault-and-battery warrant and relished the opportunity to present my perspective on Father John. It would make it a lot easier for me to bring Melanie Freeman's fraud claim if I could tell Jenny with a straight face that her brother had left me no choice.

When Heather arrived, I greeted her in the lobby as if it was a social visit.

"To what do I owe the pleasure?"

Heather's face was gray, and she avoided my eyes. She was trained at delivering bad news, and she knew how to use facial expressions and body language to set the tone.

"Can I get a cup of coffee?"

"Sure. Might be kind of stale, though."

"That's all right."

While I poured it, I made what I thought would be small talk.

"Melanie Freeman's got a job."

"Who's Melanie Freeman?"

"Melanie Freeman. The embezzlement I won at prelim."

No expression.

"You said you'd give me a chance to find her a job before you recharged it."

I handed her the coffee and she stared into the cup.

"Okay, I'll drop it."

Her answer shocked me.

"Just like that?"

"Just like that."

She wore the same solemn, wooden expression I recalled from the night she broke up with me. I led her into my office, and she took a client chair, blowing on the coffee while I shut the door.

"So, what's up?"

"Did you read the *Post* today?"

"Sure."

"There was a death in Del Ray. I think you might have known her."

For the first time in my life, I had a sensation that I'd always considered a product of fiction. The hair stood up on the back of my neck.

She waited as I slowly retrieved the paper from the wastebasket, separated the Metro section and spread it open across my desk. My vision became hazy and seemed to tunnel, my mind spinning to a bad place.

"What killed her?"

"Hard to tell. Her roommate found her. She'd been dead since the night before. Indications of arsenic. I'm sorry, Joth."

"Arsenic?"

"Acute arsenic poisoning. It's only preliminary, but I don't think our analysis will change. They found a partially eaten apple near her body. They're testing it now. Would have killed her pretty quick, if that's any consolation."

"It was in the apple?"

"Probably. Organic arsenic in small amounts is natural occurring in apples. She wouldn't have noticed anything odd in the taste."

My mind worked robotically to manufacture a response.

"You arrest anybody?"

"It's early. We're still trying to get a handle on it. The roommate clammed up."

She let me have the time I needed, and I don't know how long it was until I spoke again.

"Can I see her?"

"Of course. I can take you down."

"No, just make a call, will you?"

She scratched at the top of her head.

"Look, I know you were close, Joth. Do you know where she might have gotten the poison?"

I stared at her for some time, fighting conflicting but equally ugly emotions.

"You aren't suggesting she killed herself?"

"You know anybody with a motive?"

Heather could be a hard woman when the need arose. She knew Jenny didn't commit suicide. She wanted to push me off balance to see if I'd finger my former client.

"Anybody with a grudge against her?"

"No."

She nodded.

Then she resorted to the direct approach.

"You had a client. He said she kicked him. Lost a testicle."

"Chris Barkley?"

"He had a motive."

I pinched the bridge of my nose.

"You don't know what you're talking about."

"You know I have to ask."

"Then ask him."

"Somebody will. I want to know what you think."

"He didn't actually lose his testicle, you know."

"I understand she broke up with you."

I tilted my head and looked up at her.

"I'm sorry Joth," she said softly. "Somebody has to ask the tough questions."

"And you thought it would be better coming from you than a homicide cop?"

"I've got a job to do."

"She didn't really dump me. I was too old for her."

As I spoke these words, I knew they were a lie. The barrier between us wasn't twelve years, an arbitrary number. But it was something equally beyond my control. I had known her when she was Jade.

"She just wanted some space. It wasn't that serious anyway."

"It's hard for me to imagine who would do this."

"Is it? Last time her name came up, you said she was practically a call girl."

"That was a mistake. Did she work for Dan?"

"You know she did."

"Does this have anything to do with the people we talked about? Or the advice I gave you?"

This was her way of working around to Irish Dan, a person she always thought of whenever a crime was committed in Arlington. She deserved an honest answer.

"It might. Did you talk to Dan?"

"I have people over there now, running that down. He's too smart to say much."

"I'm sure you'll come up with no shortage of suspects."

I stood up.

"Is there anything else?"

She thought about it as she got up.

"I'll be looking for someone familiar with arsenic. A doctor, maybe a scientist or a lab tech. Somebody who understands the difficulty of detecting it in an apple."

"You never stop working, do you?"

"Joth, I'm really sorry."

I nodded and kneaded my upper lip between my teeth.

"I'm going to head down to the morgue. Do me a favor and make that call."

"Joth, we'll investigate it out of my office."

My head snapped. I knew what that meant. It was an election year and Heather wasn't going to let herself get bogged down with rumors about her personal relationship with a defense lawyer with a reputation for sordid clients and hardball tactics.

"You're going to sit on this?"

"We're going to take our time. We're going to be sure. That's in your best interests too, Joth."

The case would stay open on the back burner pending "further developments," which would only come after the election, if they came at all. And Jennifer Tedesco's killer would walk the earth, unmolested.

"What's in my best interest is knowing the name of the person who killed Jenny. If you don't find him, I will."

She glanced at her feet and nodded slowly before turning to leave. I knew she had gotten what she wanted. She always did.

***

On second thought, I didn't go to the morgue. I didn't see the point. I had known Jenny as a vibrant young woman in a green dress. I knew enough about arsenic to know that Heather had lied to me. Jenny's death may have been quick, but it would have been grim and gruesome and the face I'd see in the morgue was not the one I wanted to remember. Science doesn't lie.

Instead of immersing myself in the darkness of the morgue, I walked up the narrow, dimly lit stairs to DP's second floor office. I found him standing in the middle of the room, his bare feet shoulder width apart on the hardwood floor. He was engaged in the stylized weight shifting from one foot to the other that he called "the Bear," an exercise he did to prepare for his T'ai Chi routine.

He turned enough to acknowledge me with a nod, then resumed his rhythmic swaying, eyes half shut, his bantam weight sunk down into his bended knees.

DP's profession had taken him into some dark corners, and he had a rare knowledge of criminal instrumentalities.

"What can you tell me about arsenic?"

He stopped immediately. With a quick look at me, he stepped behind his desk, and sat down. DP was instinctively suspicious. It was what made him good at his job.

"Depends on what you want to know," he said.

I knew that arsenic had several legitimate industrial uses.

"Where would I go if I needed to buy some?"

He peered at me intently.

"How much you need?"

I took the chair across from him.

"No, I don't want to buy it; I just want to know."

"Want to know what?"

The dingy windows and general stuffiness gave the room the feel of a converted storeroom, which it probably was. I was beginning to sweat. I took a deep breath.

"How much do you need to kill a 120-pound woman in good health."

"Why do you need to know that?"

The morning's newspaper had been folded up and tossed in a wastebasket within arm's reach of where I sat. I snatched it, pulled out the Metro section and turned to the Local Digest. I marked it with a pen and flipped it across to him. He read it quickly, then began stroking his jaw. After a moment's consideration, he read the blurb again, more carefully, then looked up at me sadly.

"Maybe a farm on the Eastern Shore."

"You know anyone?"

"No."

"What about closer to home?"

He looked again at the Metro page, then tilted his head toward the low, beamed ceiling and rubbed his shiny head.

"I've known you for a long time, Joth, but I shouldn't be telling you this stuff."

"This is on the clock."

He waved the back of a hand at me, dismissing that notion.

"Inorganic arsenic. That's the stuff that can kill you. It's restricted, but you can get it. It's used in small quantities for a lot of things."

"Such as?"

He looked at the ceiling and rotated his shoulders.

"It's used to make phosphate-based fertilizers. Try one of the bigger landscapers or garden centers around here."

Garden centers? Where had I heard that before?

Back in my office, I was scrolling through a Google search of local garden centers, when I came upon a name that rang a bell: Braddock Road Garden Center. After a few moments, I made the connection. It wasn't someone who knew about arsenic. It was someone who knew that Gala loved apples.

I called the number for Braddock Road and asked for sales. A cheerful woman's voice answered.

"Hi, Lew Archer, here, Archer Landscaping Services?"

I paused, as if waiting for her to recognize the name.

"Do you manufacture and package your own phosphate-based fertilizer? I'm looking for a new supplier."

"We do, but not for wholesale. You'd have to buy it at the retail price."

I followed through with the pretext, getting the price details, then told her I'd get back to her. I hung up and called back to ask the main receptionist what time Chris Barkley got off work.

Later that afternoon, I was waiting in the parking lot near his aging pickup when he came outside.

The gravel lot was full of SUV's. It was springtime, and the homeowners of Northern Virginia were descending like locusts on the garden supply and home improvement outlets inside the Beltway, picking up yard art, flowering plants and koi for their ponds.

I watched Chris approach in my side view mirror, then hopped out as he bent to unlock his door.

"Hello, Chris. Coffee?"

I handed him one of the two vente Starbucks I'd bought twenty minutes earlier, then walked around and settled into the passenger seat.

"I thought you were moving to the islands."

The odors of sweat and stale KFC combined to create a revolting stench inside his truck.

"Working on it, Mr. Proctor."

My question might have irked him. Or maybe it was just me, getting in his face with no warning. It was hard to distinguish Barkley's nerves from his natural anxiety. He knew I wanted something, and he probably knew what it was.

"Something wrong?"

"Jade's dead."

"Yeah, I heard."

He flexed his hands around the rim of the wheel.

"I'm sorry. Everybody's shocked."

"Who told you?"

"You know, people at the place."

"Cops talk to you?"

"No. Will they?"

"Of course, they will. You never got over her, did you?"

He looked both horrified and shocked.

"What do you mean?"

"What do you think they're going to talk to you about?"

"I don't know."

He answered as if he'd never considered the question.

"They don't like unsolved murders in Arlington. Either they'll find out who did it or you'll be the patsy."

He stared straight ahead as this reality sunk in.

"Where did you get the arsenic, Chris?"

"What arsenic?"

He asked with wide-eyed surprise. He was still a child in so many ways, still incapable of dissembling. Then, suddenly, the darkness cleared, and I saw the blinding light.

"The arsenic you gave to Track."

His face fell into confusion, like a boy who suddenly realizes the consequences of a trivial mischief.

"He said it was for the reenactors."

"Reenactors? What are you talking about?"

"It's true. They rub it on their weapons to make 'em look old."

"But you didn't believe that hogwash. You knew what he was going to do with it. You knew Gala loved apples and that Track wanted her gone."

He nodded, as tears formed in his eyes.

"What did he pay you, Chris?"

"He said he could get me some Oxy."

"Oxycodone? Did he get it for you?"

"Yeah, he did."

"When was that?"

"Just a couple of days ago. I lose track."

After a long sob, he looked up.

"I haven't seen him since."

It took him another moment to gather himself.

"Mr. Joth," he said miserably, putting a hand on my arm as I reached for the door handle. "What should I tell the cops?"

"Tell them anything you want."

Chapter Twenty-Five

Southern Justice

I knew where to find Track. May 24th was Confederate Memorial Day, when the true believers gathered in Old Town to celebrate the day the volunteers left Alexandria to join the army in 1861. The statue of a contemplative volunteer in Confederate garb that stands in the center of the intersection of South Prince and Washington Streets is called "Appomattox." The soldier's back is turned toward the nation's capital and the names of the honored dead are engraved on the pedestal.

By late afternoon, the intersection was crowded with Southern sympathizers, locals, and the curious, jamming up traffic in all directions. Horns blared and protesters and counter-protesters chanted and taunted from the adjacent streets. The presence of protesters had increased in recent years, but their appearance had only fired up the pride of the defenders of Alexandria's antebellum heritage. They had turned out in force. Among these, was a battalion of reenacters, dressed in the ghostly gray of Robert E. Lee's army and posed in battle-ready ranks on the south side of the intersection.

I made my way into the crowd in time to catch the rousing, closing words of the final speech of the day. A gray haired, bearded gentlemen, dressed in the silken finery of Jefferson Davis, one arm raised in benediction, was completing an impassioned recital of Southern conceptions of honor and chivalry, while invoking a dream that was as dead as Lee himself.

"Remember!" He cried. "Above all, remember the dead and what they stood for!"

It was dusk, and a rosy sunset tinted the buildings and the Stars and Bars battle flags on each corner of the intersection. Track was easy to spot as the gathering broke up, head and shoulders above the cohort of faux-Confederates in the departing crowd.

As he left alone, I trailed him. After a few blocks, the crowd dissipated into knots of two or three and individuals moving alone. At St. Asaph Street, I called his name. He turned and stopped when he saw me.

"I thought that was you."

He seemed perplexed, or perhaps chagrined to be caught in his costume.

"What are you doing down here?"

"Curious, I guess. About honoring the Cause."

He studied me for signs of insincerity or cynicism. Apparently satisfied, he nodded.

"I didn't know you were even aware of the Cause."

"There's a lot of things you don't know about me."

He stuck out his hand and I shook it.

"No hard feelings?"

I didn't exactly nod, but I didn't shake my head, either.

Track was a man of the present who paradoxically found comfort in the past; a man of action who did not dwell on his daily victories or defeats. The insurance proceeds had been distributed and the viatical had been paid out to those with an interest. There was nothing left for him to think about. "We both did what we had to do, Joth."

"How can we ever do anything less?"

We continued walking in the direction if the river.

"And I got a sweet boat out of it, too."

"Yup. Jake loved to show it off. Beautiful little boat."

I chuckled.

"Did you ever go through the collection of junk Jake left on board?"

"No, I just wanted to get rid of it, to tell you the truth."

"You know, Track, I found quite a collection of Civil War memorabilia in a locker under one of the cushions in the cabin."

He stopped and turned to look at me, waiting for more.

"Yeah, Jake had some of the papers of a local Confederate general. Looking through them is what inspired me to come down here."

"Which Confederate general?"

"Some guy named Corse. A guy from right here in Alexandria."

"Montgomery Corse?"

"Might be. Yeah, I think it is. Commanded a brigade under Pickett?"

"What kind of papers?"

"Oh, I don't know. I just leafed through them. Looks like they might be his personal journals and correspondence. Probably worth something."

"They look original?"

"I didn't look that closely. Maybe you'd know where I could have the stuff valued?"

Track stroked his bearded chin.

"I could help you there, Joth."

He paused and his chest swelled with pride.

"You know, I'm descended from Monty Corse."

"No!"

"He was in Pickett's Charge."

"Was he? Well, I sailed down from the marina. Got the boat tied up right down at the end of King Street. You want to take a look?"

Track scanned the sky, dubiously. It was slightly overcast with a steady breeze from the north. The sun was going down and it was chilly, but dressed in his officer's wool cloak, he was prepared for it.

"I'll have to check with Mo."

As he took his phone out of his pocket, I smirked.

"Just like Jake, huh?"

"What do you mean?"

"He was whipped, too."

"I'm not whipped."

"That's what Carter said. But he knew the truth. He couldn't do anything without checking with Maureen first. Of course, she has the money, right?"

Track put the phone back in his coat.

I'd left the *Southern Patriot* tied bow and stern to an isolated dock behind a construction site. On a similar chilly spring night in 1862, General George McClellan and 100,000 Union troops had embarked on transports bound for the Virginia peninsula from this spot, but now there wasn't a soul in sight.

Once aboard, I pointed down the short companionway into the little cabin, where a sheaf of papers, held together by a large binder clip, were visible under the cabin light on one of the bunks.

The Papers of Montgomery Dent Corse are publicly available at the Alexandria public library, where I had made the copies. Track was now sorting through them with the intense concentration I associated with twelve-year-old boys and glossy magazines.

As he settled on the opposite bunk to study this find, I quietly cast off. The *Southern Patriot* floated out into the river. I raised the main and watched it fill. As we reached gently out into the channel, his head poked up from the companionway.

"What's going on?"

"I thought we'd take a little sail. It's a beautiful evening."

His face screwed up.

"This isn't the right time for it. I've got things to do."

"I thought you'd want a little time to look through those papers."

He came up and sat in the cockpit across from me. The level rays of the setting sun burnished the water in the direction of Alexandria.

"You don't need them, do you, Joth?"

"Well, you gave them to me. They came with the boat, right?"

He took a moment to scan the horizon.

"You think I could take them with me, make copies?"

I didn't answer. It was early in the season and there was no one on the river. I raised the jib, and we ran south before the steady breeze, passing under an arch of the Woodrow Wilson Bridge that spanned the Beltway across the Potomac.

For a time, we settled into the moment. Yellow squares of light blinked on in windows along the shores of Maryland and Virginia and Track seemed content to enjoy a pleasurable evening sail.

"What exactly happened to Carter?"

Track sucked in a lung full of air, as if he knew a debrief was coming.

"Is somebody at risk of prosecution?"

"My guy with Metro police told me his file's closed—accidental death. Heather won't touch you."

He nodded thoughtfully.

"You're still my attorney, right?"

"Of course."

"Confidentiality prevails?"

"What you tell me will never leave this boat."

He gestured with his chin down the companionway.

"I want those papers."

"Consider them yours."

He thought about it and nodded decisively.

"I told you, Jake was drinking, and he fell."

"How come you didn't call 911?"

"It would have looked bad, Joth. Me holding the policy and all. It was a snap decision. It would have looked bad for you, too."

The wind shifted slightly to the west. I nodded and adjusted the tiller to port, keeping the boat ahead of the wind.

"You keep your mouth shut and it'll pass. They've got no evidence and suspicions don't get indictments."

"I hope you're right. Terrible thing. I really liked the guy. Everybody did."

He stretched his legs across to the opposite banquette and folded his arms. Now that the sun was down, it grew dark quickly and a chill came with the breeze. He pulled his cloak tightly around him.

"Maybe we ought to head back, huh?"

"Let's push down beyond that point, and I'll bring her about."

The river had turned from purple to black.

"It's getting cold out here."

I looked at Track.

"We've still got a few things to get straight."

"Like what? Sounds like everything fell into place."

"Did she know what you were planning to do?"

"Who? Mo?"

He smirked.

"I don't share my plans with anyone."

"You're a very careful guy."

"She's better off this way. With me, instead of Jake."

He laughed and flicked a finger at the star on his collar.

"I'm a general. Jake was just a colonel."

"And Jenny?"

Track dropped his eyes and grimaced.

"I'm sorry about what happened to her. I really am."

"Yeah? What do you know about it?"

He shrugged.

"Just what I heard."

"Heard from who?"

He opened his hands in a resigned gesture.

"Just what's going around, you know. Scuttlebutt. I was shocked."

"Sure, you were shocked. You must have been. Because the arsenic was meant for Gala."

He looked away and squirmed.

"What are you talking about?"

"Gala owed you money, Track. We won't get into why. So, you asked her to make a call, and she did, but that didn't end the problem, because you still owed her cash under the viatical. You were just too tied up with her, weren't you?"

"Whoever told you that is lying. Come on, Joth. Get me back on land."

"The blackmail, the Oxy . . . in the end, she was just too unreliable. Of course, she's too unreliable to be much of a witness against you, but you don't take any chances, do you, Track?"

"Listen, Joth. I know this is about Jade, but I heard she'd moved in with you. She shouldn't have been around."

I looked at him carefully, just able to make out his features in the gathering darkness. "Her name was Jenny."

"Sure. Of course, it was. But it wasn't my fault."

"Not your fault?'

"That's right. Look, Joth, you did your job, and you did it right. That's why I gave you this boat, remember? It was an accident. Let's leave it at that. I got things to do."

"An accident? Because you murdered the wrong woman?"

Track recoiled at the blunt charge, but he didn't back away from it.

"They'll never get me for that."

Until that moment, I could have tacked the boat, returned him to the pier and gone home, but now the western horizon glowed blood red. "Is that what you think?"

"You said so yourself."

Unburdened and emboldened, he slowly leaned back and puffed his chest.

"DC's dropped it. The Commonwealth Attorney's dropped it. You did a nice job tying everybody up. Now I can go back to doing what I do best, which is making money."

"You think that's the end of it?"

Track smiled smugly.

"The only person who knows what happened is you, and you're my lawyer. Yeah, you fixed it good. We'll both come out of this all right."

I wasn't surprised that he believed this, but his arrogance took my breath away.

"Yeah. So, tell me about Montgomery Corse."

He straightened up and seemed to preen, glad for a chance to indulge his family pride.

"My great, great grandfather. Led Pickett's Charge up Cemetery Ridge."

I laughed.

"You'll have to check those papers Jake left aboard. Corse was assigned to Pickett's division all right, but he was in southern Virginia, 200 miles from Gettysburg, in July of 1863."

Track stared at me and then looked away, insulted at my challenge to the bedrock family myth that he treasured above all others.

"Well, that's just wrong."

We were in the middle of the channel, moving steadily before the wind. He didn't seem shocked or horrified, and I wondered if he'd known the truth all along.

"It's all right there in black and white, Track."

"That's not what my daddy taught us."

"Then he was a liar, just like you."

He looked up sharply and glared. I'd had enough.

"You lied to everyone all the time, and it got so easy you didn't know the difference anymore. It got so you could even lie to yourself about life and death."

"That's not true!"

"True? Lying is how you make your living. I may be the only one who knows the whole truth about you, Track." Then I paused and added, "And I'm the only one who can do anything about it."

Track didn't move. I'd laid a lot on him and he wasn't used to that. I wasn't used to it either. But I felt liberated and emboldened by the power of words I had never allowed myself to speak before.

I stepped forward and impulsively reached under the hatch to the handy place where Jake Carter had stored his loaded cavalry revolver. I cocked it and pointed it at

Track as I resumed the helm. He looked at me in shock, until a scowl slowly took over his entire face.

"She's not worth it, Joth. She was a stripper."

I was enraged by his callousness, his inability to separate the person from the dollar sign that person represented to him, and I acted on this. "She was worth twice what you are. Tell her I said so when you see her."

I pumped a single bullet into the left side of his chest. His head flew backward with the impact and he grunted. That was the last sound Frank Racker ever made.

I waited half a minute while I scanned the empty horizon, then I took a breath and checked his pulse. He wasn't dead, but he soon would be. The bullet had made a substantial hole, but the powder burn had staunched the initial flow of blood. His face had turned a livid white.

After throwing on the automatic pilot to keep us ahead of the wind, I took Jake's bedroll from inside the cabin, pulled it over Track's head, and zipped his still warm body inside. Then I took the extra anchor and chain from the starboard locker and wrapped it tightly around what was now a limp package and tied it off with several half-hitches. I scanned the river again, then rolled this human debris off the port gunwale and watched it sink like a stone.

As it disappeared into the blackness, I took a gulp of air. The blood that had pounded almost audibly in my temples subsided and I examined my quivering hand on the tiller.

I brought the little sloop about and switched on the running lights, steadying myself as I began beating up the river toward the security of the marina. Under the Wilson Bridge, I dropped Carter's revolver into the wine dark water and didn't look back. The boat cleaved silently through the empty river, and the lights of the Capitol sparkled in the distance. My mouth was as dry as leather, and as I pushed on, a cold, forsaken feeling germinated in the pit of my stomach and began to swell. I told myself that there was now one less predator taking easy money from vulnerable people, and in the world I wanted to live in, that was a good thing. But I had assumed the awesome responsibilty of unappealable judgment. Anxiety and dread overwhelmed my sense of righteousness and justification.

After a few minutes of uneasy sailing, I was startled by a sudden flash from over my shoulder that for a snapshot moment illuminated the river and both shorelines. More lighting followed, and then the low, ominous rumble of thunder. The next bolt sustained itself through a series of pulsing flashes and the ensuing thunder echoed up and down the Potomac. The wind suddenly veered and strengthened, starting a chop on the water and signaling the front of a storm that approached on rolling, roiling clouds from the south. I reacted promptly, dropping both sails. As I engaged the engine, a jagged bolt of lightning zigzagged across the evening sky. The thunder that followed was closer now and it boomed like cannon fire. The river churned with whitecaps.

The storm hit with the shock and power of an explosion. The wind shrieked through the halyards and stays and blew the waves into troughs, battering the little sloop like a cork cast adrift on the ocean. The rain came down in sheets, drenching me to the skin. I fought the helm the whole way in.

Finally, back to the marina, I secured *Southern Patriot* into her slip and quickly furled the sails as the pelting rain lashed the cockpit. Exhausted, I shook the rain out of my eyes, looked down at my shaking hands and considered what I had done. Then I hurried up the dock to the sanctuary of my car.

As I drove slowly home, Heather's image appeared between the flashes of lightning like an avenging angel. I shook this vision off, but I couldn't shake the question that accompanied it: what furies were riding on that raging wind?

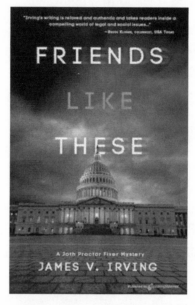

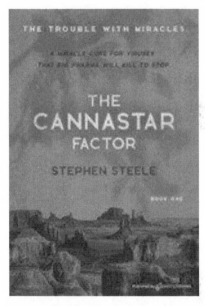

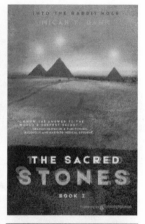

On Sale Now!

JOHN DeDAKIS'S
LARK CHADWICK MYSTERIES

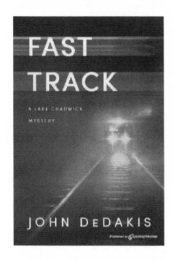

**For more information
visit:**

Sign up for free and bargain books

Join the Speaking Volumes mailing list

Text

ILOVEBOOKS

to 22828 **to get started.**

Message and data rates may apply.

Made in the USA
Middletown, DE
26 May 2021

40465559R00203